YOU DON'T EVEN KNOW ME

Also by Sharon G. Flake

The Skin I'm In

Bang!

Who Am I Without Him?

Money Hungry

Begging for Change

YOU DON'T EVEN KNOW ME

STORIES AND POEMS ABOUT BOYS

SHARON G. FLAKE

Disney • Jump at the Sun
Los Angeles   New York

Copyright © 2010 by Sharon G. Flake

All rights reserved. Published by Disney • Jump at the Sun, an imprint of Disney Book Group. No part of this book may be reproduced or transmitted in any form or by any means, electronic or mechanical, including photocopying, recording, or by any information storage and retrieval system, without written permission from the publisher. For information address Disney • Jump at the Sun, 125 West End Avenue, New York, New York 10023.

First Hardcover Edition, February 2010

First Paperback Edition, July 2011

10 9 8 7 6 5 4 3 2 1

FAC-025438-18292

This book is set in 12-point Janson Text LT Pro/Fontspring

Printed in the United States of America

ISBN 978-1-368-01943-9

Library of Congress Control Number for Hardcover: 2005047434
ISBN 978-1-368-01945-3

Visit www.DisneyBooks.com

SUSTAINABLE
FORESTRY
INITIATIVE

Certified Chain of Custody
Promoting Sustainable Forestry
www.sfiprogram.org
SFI-01054
The SFI label applies to the text stock

To my parents, Langston Hughes, and my neighborhood family, who showed me how beautiful I was; who reminded me what a great gift my neighborhood was to the planet, who taught me that the way I spoke was music to the ears and that it was okay to simply be me—a little black girl from the inner city of Philadelphia.

To all who read and find my words, I give you the light that they all lit up in me. go forth and shine.

TABLE OF CONTENTS

YOU DON'T EVEN KNOW ME

I sit in your class
I play by the rules
I'm young
I'm fly
I'm black.
So of course I think I'm cool.
Geometry is my thing,
Physics is just a breeze.
So it bothered me last week
When you said I should be happy with that C.
You know,
I've been wondering lately,
Trying to figure out just how it could be
That you're around me so often
And still don't know a thing about me.
You

See me on TV,
Marching in the band,
Then you flick the channel
And there I am again,
Cuffs on my hands,
A coat over my head,
The news anchor warning that I'm someone you
    should dread.
The police say I'm a menace,
That you should be on the alert.
The nightly news recounts all the people they say
    I've hurt.
The mayor says I'm a threat,
Psychologists call me depressed,
Bloggers can't figure out what's up with me, so they
    make up all the rest.
You know,
I've been wondering lately,
Trying to figure out just how it could be
That you can see me so often
And still don't know a thing about me.
I live next door to you,
You see me on the bus.
Sometimes you even tell me just be quiet, child—hush.
Then I'm out with my boys—

Two, five, or even ten—
It's funny when that happens, you don't seem to
    know me then.
I'm just another black boy,
A threatening, scary sight.
A tall, black, eerie shadow
Moving toward you late at night.
You know,
I've been wondering lately,
Trying to figure out just how it could be
That you could talk to me so often
And still not know a thing about me.
We hang on the corner together,
Holding up the wall,
I tell you about my dreams,
You just wanna talk basketball.
I pull out my plans
Detailing the cities I'll rebuild one day,
Swearing
That people will know my name across the USA.
You tell me to quit fronting,
You ask who I think I am,
Pretending
That I'm better than you know I really am.
You talk about my house,

The clothes I wear sometimes,
Then you really hit me with what's been on your mind.
You know,
I've been wondering lately,
Trying to figure out just how it could be
That we call each other brother,
And you still don't know a thing about me.

Last night I had a dream
I flew right past the stars.
No one was holding their pocketbooks,
Or double-locking cars.
I chatted with the moon,
Calculated the circumference of the sun.
Then right before I awoke
I decided to take a run.
I ran across the Milky Way,
Stole a peek at Saturn's ring,
Hip-hopped across the Universe.
I was me.
I could do anything,
So I dived into a million black holes,
Rested my feet on the north and south poles.
Slipped into my mother's dreams,
My daddy's nightmares, too.

We talked about my future and the great things that I
    will do.
But dreams don't last forever
And night turns into day,
Where people who don't even know you
Try to block tomorrow's way.
But nothing can ever stop me,
Keep me
From what's mine.
The stars
On fire
Inside me
Shining
Refining
Reminding
Me
That only I define me
And
The brightness of my destiny.

SCARED TO DEATH

"**D**ON'T THROW UP. Not here. Not now. Not on her," he told himself. Then he swallowed the Froot Loops that had snuck back into his mouth, no matter how hard he tried to make 'em stay down.

The preacher asked him again: "Do you, Tow-Kaye, take this woman to be your lawfully wedded wife, to have and to hold, from this day forward until death do you part?"

"I guess."

Cindella stared at him, then at her belly. Her father, sitting in the first row, cleared his throat. So did the pastor. Tow-Kaye thought about what his father told him this morning. "You ain't gotta marry her, or nobody, for no reason, ever." He changed his answer. "Yes. I take her to be my wife," he said, still wondering if maybe his father was right: A sixteen-year-old boy "don't need to be getting married."

"And do you, Cindella, take Tow-Kaye to be your lawfully wedded husband?"

She giggled, which made the women in the church lean over and say they knew she was too darn young to be getting married. Cindella saw a few of them out the corner of her eyes—whispering. She couldn't understand why people were so upset. Marriage was a good thing, wasn't it? Tow-Kaye and her paid for their own rings, didn't they? And they were going to finish high school, and work together at the same restaurant this summer. What else did people want? "I do . . . take him to be my husband," she said, looking over at Tow-Kaye. Smiling and kissing him before he kissed her.

She wanted to jump the broom after the ceremony. Not him. He thought it would make him look stupid, hopping over a broom in front of his boys. So they walked up the aisle, hand in hand—her wearing a beaded ivory gown and him wearing a black tux with a matching cummerbund, when he would have been perfectly fine in a pair of new jeans.

"This the twenty-first century, you don't have to do nothing you don't want to," his father said to him last night after his friends stopped blowing up his cell, asking if he was crazy getting married at his age. So he was kind of glad his father wasn't here, because he figured his dad would be able to tell for sure that he was having second thoughts—scared to death, really.

When they headed up the aisle, behind the bridesmaids and best man, her friends waved at her like she was a movie star walking the red carpet.

"Stop! Wait! Let us take your picture."

Cindella stopped. She held on to him tighter than a blind man to a cane. "He yours now," her best friend, Raquel, said, walking into the aisle, taking too many pictures. "I'ma be next."

A woman too old to stand up told Tow-Kaye to smile. "And look happy."

Tow-Kaye wanted to run. To ditch Cindella and his tux and get out of there. But he didn't, because he loved her. Loved her since he was four years old, when he moved onto her block. Up until fourth grade he called her Cinderella. She had big, light brown eyes and short wavy hair that felt like feathers when he touched it. He kissed her for the first time when they were seven; gave her a yellow plastic ring when they were ten. On his thirteenth birthday he gave her all of his birthday money and said what was his was hers. He wanted to tell her how much he loved her, right there in front of everybody. But if he did, he might just throw up. So he kept walking.

His best friend, Mario, got to him first. They hugged each other. "This is nuts, man. Stupid. But you stuck now."

Tow-Kaye's mother got to him next—kissing him. Dragging him over to the reception line, not noticing that inside he was already calling it quits.

The vestibule was draped in their school colors— purple and yellow—a gift from their friends. Tow-Kaye waved at his boys. Her friends picked at her dress and fussed over her hair. Then four of his friends slid their fingers across their throats and sliced. It was a joke. He knew that. But he didn't laugh. He kept moving.

Tow-Kaye shook hands with the first guest in the receiving line, then looked at Cindella and smiled. The sun was shining through the stained glass windows, turning her gown mauve, amber, and honeysuckle; making the stones in her tiara glow blue. That's what made him kiss her. Made his lips stay on her lips for so long that his mom said they should quit it.

He rubbed her belly. "Two more months and I'll be a father." Then he rubbed his own stomach, and belched. Right before the wedding he took six tablespoons of Pepto-Bismol, but it didn't help. His stomach was still in knots.

"You look sick," his wife said, staring at the dark circles under his eyes, and his dry, cracked lips. Tow-Kaye was light brown. His skin showed everything. "You okay?" she asked.

Before he could tell her what he was thinking—that he was scared, that he didn't know if he wanted to be married—his mother walked over and squeezed his cheek. "I am so proud of you." Then she lowered her voice. "I wish he had come." She smelled his boutonniere, then turned him toward her and straightened his bow tie. "So he could have seen you standing up there . . . doing right by that girl."

His father didn't understand. Tow-Kaye had to marry her. He'd promised her. And he never broke a promise, not to Cindella.

"Okay, Mom. Let somebody else hug him." It was Cindella's mother talking. She hugged Tow-Kaye's mom, then hugged him. Other people couldn't tell how she felt about him, but he knew. She was like his dad—ticked off about the marriage. But she was better at pretending than his father was.

"This is Mrs. Dunkin," Cindella's mother said, introducing a woman to her daughter. "She lived up the street when you were little."

"What you talking about? She still little," Mrs. Dunkin said, putting a big, fat, wet kiss on Cindella's cheek, then wiping the lipstick off with her thumb, which was partially amputated.

They stood in the receiving line shaking hands and hugging people forever, it seemed. A woman handed her a twenty. A man gave him a fifty, saying, "And this ain't no honey-I-got-some-money money, this here's for you. Pocket change." The guy smiled, showing off a gold tooth in the corner of his mouth. Tow-Kaye slipped the new bill into his back pocket, hoping Cindella hadn't seen.

It was like that the rest of the time, people hugging and kissing them. Women handing her cards; men sliding him five-dollar bills. Putting twenties and fifties in his back pocket. He didn't know people did things like that. But he could use a new iPod and that new Madden game, he thought as he took Cindella by the hand and left the church, asking if anyone had a spoon. "I got some medicine I need to take."

Tow-Kaye stared out the limousine window. A hoop game was going on in the park. He played every day; most of Saturday. His dad said he could kiss that good-bye. But his mother said he didn't have to. "Marriage is compromise. You give some, you get some things too." Only Tow-Kaye wasn't so sure anymore about what marriage got you, besides a wife and a bad stomach.

He didn't know who to believe. People said such different things. "Marriage sucks—run." "Be responsible; take care of what's yours." But who's gonna take care of me? he thought. His mother always cooked for him, washed his clothes, and even made his bed. They were gonna be living with Cindella's parents now. Her mom was different. At their place, you ironed your own things. Cleaned up after your own self and took turns cleaning the bathroom and the refrigerator, too—even the men. Cindella said she would treat him just the way his mother had. "I'll do everything for you." But his boy Mario said if he believed that, then he had a dirt bike that went five thousand miles an hour that he wanted to sell to him.

"They got anything to eat in this car?" Tow-Kaye started opening up compartments and pulling out juice and snacks. He started with peanuts and was into the Doritos before the peanut bag was empty.

Cindella took the bags away. "They make your breath smell." Then she took out some of the cards and money people had given them, even though her mother said she shouldn't. He felt guilty, so he dumped his cash into her pile.

Two guys flew past their limousine on motorcycles. Tow-Kaye's father had promised him one for graduation. Cindella hated those things. He wondered if he'd have to give that up too. He opened up more compartments, pulled out crackers and cheese, sparkling red cider, and a corkscrew.

She told him to watch out for the cider. "It stains."

"You not my mother. Don't tell me what to do."

Mrs. Bentley bit her lip, to keep from saying anything she'd regret.

"Relax. You two can make it," Cindella's father said. "My parents got married at thirteen."

"You're almost sixty," his wife said. "In your mother's day, girls didn't have a future. Making babies, that was their job." She stared at Cindella. "Things are different now. Girls don't *ever* have to get married if they don't want."

"But I wanted to," Cindella said.

Her mother kicked off her lime green heels. "You wanted to. . . ." She was trying not to sound angry. "But you didn't *have* to." She looked at Tow-Kaye's hand on her daughter's stomach and asked her husband for some Tylenol. "This is my baby." She pointed to her daughter. "Our last child." Her hands covered her lips. Her eyes blinked. "She was supposed to go to college—to London; Africa. You . . . it's all messed up now." She sat straight up. "Now we have to use her college money on cribs and binkies, Similac and hospital bills. Jesus. Why us?"

His mother-in-law was the principal at their high school. Every day she'd come home telling Cindella what some teacher or janitor had said about them getting married. "It's better to be pregnant and young than pregnant, young, married, and then divorced," she heard a few teachers in the lounge say one day. Her mom agreed with them. One mistake is better than ten. And being a principal, she had seen teenagers make hundreds of mistakes. But until now, getting married wasn't one of them.

She finally broke down crying. Her husband hugged her and told her crying wasn't going to change nothing, and that his girl deserved a husband for her baby, not no boy who wanted to stand on the corner or play video games half the night. He leaned over and shook Tow-Kaye's hand. "He's more man than some men my age. He always was . . . a good kid."

Tow-Kaye tied his shoelaces, then stared out the black tinted windows. "I'm responsible. I try to do what's right, but . . ."

Her mother dug in her purse for Tylenol. "Responsible? Responsible?"

Cindella and her dad both said, "Don't say it."

"You knocked her up!" She let everything she had been thinking come out. "Pregnant and married at sixteen. Jesus Christ. What a disaster!" She closed her eyes and reminded herself that she was a principal: she knew better. She was a mother: she needed to do better. But all she could do was cry.

The limo pulled into the park and up to the conservatory. Tow-Kaye could hear the rest of the wedding party from the second limousine jumping out of the car, laughing, and heading their way. Adrina knocked on their window first. "What y'all doing in there, kissing?"

He burped and tasted peanuts, then looked at his ring and wished he could take it off—start the day all over again. "Man . . ." He said it out loud, even though he knew he shoulda kept it in his head. "This is the worst day of my life."

They stared at him. And something inside him made him say what his father wanted him to say all along. "I'm too young to be married." His stomach bubbled. "And I hate this suit." He opened the window for air. "I'm only in eleventh grade. Who gets married at my age?"

Cindella started crying. Her mother started yelling. Tow-Kaye said he was sorry, but he couldn't do this.

Her dad stepped in. "Driver, let's take a little ride through the park." He looked around the car. "What a mess." So when the car pulled off and they rode deeper into the park, where there was nothing but trails, thick tall trees, and air so clean it smelled sweet, he told the driver to stop. "Come on, boy." He opened the door and told the women to stay put.

They walked on the gravel and watched dust hug their rented shoes. "Talk to me," Cindella's dad said, loosening his gray tie.

Tow-Kaye wondered how much of the pink stuff you could take in a day. He wanted a little more, wanted to get drunk really, and he didn't even drink.

His father-in-law said it again. "Talk to me, son. You want out? You can get out."

Tow-Kaye loved Mr. Bentley. Before he ever told Cindella he loved her, he said it to her father first. Tow-Kaye's father called him every week, but he lived in California and they never did talk about much. Once he got sick with cancer and lost his job, he couldn't pay for Tow-Kaye to fly out there. Neither could his mother. Which was okay, because Tow-Kaye always had Cindella's dad. He was the one who taught him to ride a two-wheeler. He was the one who showed him how to use a hammer, how to lay concrete so it didn't crack. He went to Boy Scout meetings with Tow-Kaye and taught him to fish; told him when to wear a tie; why he shouldn't eat everything on his plate; how to act if the police ever rolled up on him; and why he always needed to have some money in his back pocket and in the bank, too.

"Be responsible for your actions. That's what you always taught me." Tow-Kaye looked at the gravel while he talked. Walked over to a tree and started pulling off the bark. "I'm trying to be . . . responsible . . . trying to do what's right."

His father-in-law was behind him, scratching the bald spot in the center of his head. "I love you . . . Gonna love you no matter what you do." He held on to his shoulder, squeezing it. Wondering if he had screwed everything up for his daughter, for his only son, too. "Maybe I'm too old to have a kid your age. . . ." He took off his jacket.

"You ain't old."

He kept talking to Tow-Kaye's back. "I know kids don't get married no more." He loosened his tie a bit more. "The first time I did it, though, I was your age. When she passed," he said, "I found another one. Emily." He listened to the birds talking to one another from tree to tree. "I don't know . . . I figured between me and Emily, and you loving Cindella and her loving you . . . it could work out right."

Tow-Kaye started walking, slow, so Mr. Bentley could keep up. And he told him what his dad had said. What his boys told him in school, at gym—on the court. Mr. Bentley helped Tow-Kaye out of his jacket. "But this ain't about them," he said, holding his coat for him. "It's about you two." He stopped. Picked up an acorn and pitched it as far as he could. Tow-Kaye did the same. They walked over to the pond—the one people fished in even though it looked like it was filled with mud. "Sit down," Mr. Bentley said, ignoring the dirt.

Tow-Kaye stood. "It's not like I don't love her." He took off his tie and cummerbund.

"Only . . . I just . . . can't . . ."

Mr. Bentley stared at the green slime moving across the water like oil. He had to, otherwise he'd cry.

"I can't stop thinking," Tow-Kaye said, swallowing in between every word. "Can't . . . shut . . . my . . . head . . . off . . . you know?" His father-in-law laughed. "Marriage is some scary stuff, man."

"No lie. I swear."

The birds got quiet. "All I can think about . . . is . . . is . . . man, I'ma be a father . . . be a husband . . . be all used up before I'm eighteen." He looked over at Mr. Bentley, then took his time sitting down next to him. "I love her . . . but I don't know. . . ." He didn't mean to cry. Didn't mean to cry so hard he wet up Mr. Bentley's shirt and got snot on his sleeve. "I wanna be married to her, you know. Wanna be with her forever and be a good dad like you, but . . ."

Mr. Bentley held him like he held Cindella when she was little. He wiped his own nose and cleared his throat and tried to figure out what to say; what to do. But all he could think about was his daughter, how hurt she'd be. And about himself, how this was all his fault. So he said it, even though he cried while he said it. "We can get it annulled. Make it like it never happened."

The sun was hot and bright, but Tow-Kaye felt a little chilled, so he put his jacket back on. "But I'm having a baby."

His father-in-law stood up. "You'll be a good dad." He looked away when he told Tow-Kaye that he'd always be welcome in their home. "Better not try staying away." He hugged him so hard the chain he'd given him for his wedding day left an impression on his chest. "I love you, boy. Forever. And nothing's ever going to change that."

They started walking, and wiping away what they didn't want their wives to see. Tow-Kaye picked up stones and skipped them up the road. He thought about food. He didn't know why. They had walked farther than they wanted; stayed longer than they should, so he knew Cindella would be upset. "Her friends are waiting to take pictures."

"Let 'em wait." Then Mr. Bentley said he'd explain everything to everyone—even her, if he wanted.

Tow-Kaye wanted to chicken out. But he couldn't.

"Naw." He put his cummerbund back on. "I'll tell her." Then he thought about something else. That's what made him stop in the middle of the road. "She's not gonna want me after this, huh?"

His father-in-law was honest. "Probably not." But he told him things between her, him, and the baby would be good. "That's just the way she is."

They kept walking. Talking. And Tow-Kaye kept asking himself, *How am I gonna live without her? How is she gonna make it without me?* "You ain't gotta marry her." He heard his father say it again.

"Fix yourself up." Mr. Bentley stopped him. He brushed a spiderweb from Tow-Kaye's hair with his fingers. He leveled Tow-Kaye's tie, then bent down to dust his shoes. When they turned the corner, the limousine was sitting there. Tow-Kaye smoothed out Mr. Bentley's jacket; made his shoes shine again. Then he rubbed dried salty tears from his own cheeks. "Bentleys don't break," his father in-law said. "She'll be alright." Only deep down inside he wasn't so sure.

"I don't know . . . we already did it now . . . got married, I mean."

He held both of Tow-Kaye's shoulders. "Don't stay just to stay. That's worse than leaving, most times."

Tow-Kaye looked up the road at Cindella, leaning

against the car, belly pocked out. He stared at her girlfriends, who had found her. He knew just what they had been saying: *Where's Tow-Kaye? Girl, he's acting up already. I knew you shouldn't a married him.*

His knees wobbled. "You think we can make it, Mr. Bentley? Think we'll be okay?"

His father-in-law took his hand. "She's my daughter, right?" he said, taking his time heading toward the limousine.

"Yes, sir."

"And you're my son, ain't you?"

Tow-Kaye squeezed his hand tight. "Yeah."

"I got your back, just like you got hers," he said. "It's gonna be hard, I won't lie to you. You'll want to run again someday, too. But all the support you need, all the love you want is here. You're with family. And family's always gonna find a way to make sure you're okay."

His boys pointed, laughing a little, watching the two men coming up the road, holding hands. The girls didn't whisper when they told Cindella she needed to go set her man straight.

Cindella started running his way. She knew he was scared. But he was hers and she loved him. And she knew he had leaving on his mind; but staying was something they were both really good at, so she figured it could work, had to. So she ignored her friends, the hard gravel between her toes, and her mother saying she'd ruin her gown.

Cinderella. That's what he thought when he saw her coming toward him, brown and beautiful.

"I love you," he said, holding her tight. "You're my wife."

"I love you too," she said, right before he kissed her, right before the sun turned the stones in her crown the color of the ring he gave her in fifth grade—golden yellow with flecks of red.

JUST SAY IT

Put it in a text
Say it with your tongue
My boys might not believe it
But I know I'm the only one
Yours
Forever
Always
A boy who became a man
The one who said he'd die before he'd hold some
    stupid girl's hand
They say you're not so pretty
They ask what I see in you
I've explained a million times
I was born loving you
So
I'll put it in a text

I'll say it with my tongue
My boys may not believe it
But I know you're the one
Mine
Forever
Always
A girl who understands
That a boy who *never* learns to love
Will *never* be a man.

GETTIN' EVEN

HE'S GOT A KNIFE. A BIG ONE.

"If . . . if . . . ahhhh . . ." he says, almost stabbing me in the back.

I turn the corner, trip over a beer bottle and a bum, jump up and keep running. My left leg cramps. My arms hurt. But if I stop, I'm dead.

"Who . . . who . . . you think you are. Knocking on my door. A-a-accusing me," Melvin yells, chasing after me.

I've been running for five blocks. And I still have three more to go. I don't think I'll make it . . . home . . . to my grandparents' house. Not without getting cut.

And it's like he can run forever, even though I'm way younger than he is. But somebody killed my grandfather. I just wanna know who.

I fly up the street faster than a hot motorcycle; feel my

sneaker come off and pieces of glass sticking to my feet like sprinkles on a cake. I cross myself, because this might be it. Then all of a sudden he stops. Just like that. And sits on some steps, wiping sweat and giving me the finger.

I can't go no further either. I sit down just a few houses up, ready to die if I have to. "He . . . he . . . I liked him . . . your grandfather," the guy shouts, holding his chest. "That the only reason you still living."

I'm breathing so hard I have to hold my chest too—hurts too bad otherwise. But my grandfather didn't raise no fool, so I start walking away fast, toward home, even though I still don't know who shot him.

I'm not on the block two minutes before Kareem asks me if the store is open. Before I can tell him, he asks where my sneaker is. "Gone," I say, staring at my bloody toes.

Kareem's house has the most steps on the block: twenty-two. He's sitting on the top one, squirting me with his water gun. "I'm coming with you. To open up the store," he says, standing.

I'm wet and tired. I need a shower. And time to get the store set up, I tell him. So he shoots me in the back of my head and stays where he is.

When I get up the street my legs are still shaking, so I sit down at the curb in front of my grandfather's store. They killed him in there. It happens a lot in this neighborhood, so the police are taking their time figuring out who did it. The neighbors put flowers and teddy bears out front, and spray-painted his name on the pavement outside the place, so they think they've done their part.

My grandmother and me argue a lot over this store. She wants it shut down. So instead of going inside the house where she is, I go in through the garage—his store. There's a shower in the back.

Once I'm clean and back in the clothes I had on earlier, I start putting cookies and candy in jars. I bought this stuff with my own money, since *she* won't give me any. But as soon as I unpack the Oreos and Twizzlers, here she comes, pointing at me with that cane.

"I told you what I wanted you to do, right?"

"Yes, ma'am."

"So just do it."

"No."

"Didn't he get shot? Didn't they just walk into this here store," she says, stabbing the floor with her cane, "and shoot him dead?"

"Yes, ma'am, but—"

"Then shut it down. Today."

"I . . ."

"Don't sass me. And don't think I don't know what you been doing out there . . . behind my back."

I stand over her. "I been doing just what you did. Going after *them*," I say, kicking the stool so hard one of the legs cracks.

She scratches underneath her wig, then straightens it. Then takes a pinch of snuff out the bag and sticks it between her orange lips; shoving it between her gums with her tongue. "You do what I did and . . . You not from around here, boy. Quit doing things like that . . . please."

After my granddad died a few months ago, my grandmother sat at the window every day and yelled at guys walking by. "You know my husband? Who shot him?" Or she would be at church—her friends would tell my mom—asking boys my age what they knew about the killing. She quit doing that after I came three weeks ago. Didn't want to make me no target, she said. But I just took over where she left off, only in my own way. Now she says for me to quit it, before something bad happens to me, too. I usually do exactly what I'm told. But not lately. Lately I feel like getting even. Paying back. Only I guess I need to be smarter. Going empty-handed doesn't make any sense. I'm not sure why I thought it would.

My granddad didn't make any money in this store. Nothing cost more than a dollar and a half, and lots of time kids got candy for free. How could anyone hurt an old man like that? And everybody who says they loved him keeps quiet about who did it. Now my grandmother is telling me to let sleeping dogs lie, and shut down the store. That's not right. They got the money, even the shoes off his feet. Now they get the store—everything he was working for—if we close it.

My parents, my uncles and aunts want it shut down too. The neighborhood's bad. The people are getting what they deserve, they say—no place for their kids to buy candy or soda or to hang out when it gets hot. I'm fourteen. And I've never spent a full summer at home. *Here* in his store is where I like to be. They're wrong for trying to take it away from me.

My grandmother and I keep going at it. Before I know it, she's doing what she did yesterday, asking for her inhaler. "You alright? You okay?" I say, coming back from the house with it.

"Help me to that chair, baby," she says, holding on to me and her throat at the same time.

This is what happened three p.m. yesterday, right before she ended up in the emergency room. I don't want her dying because of me. So I give in, right after she sits down and can't get up for a whole hour. Then I put her to bed, and watch over her for thirty minutes. I say it again:

I'll close up the store. Her breathing gets better then. "But I'm staying with you all summer," I say, swinging a bat my grandfather kept at the store for protection. "Let 'em come after me, too, if they want. I got something for them."

After she's asleep, I go back to my granddad's place. Kareem's waiting there.

"Y'all open?"

"Go home, Kareem. We closed, for good."

He walks in anyhow.

"But what you gonna do with all them cookies?" His tongue sticks out the side of his mouth. "And how 'bout those?" He's pointing to the Slim Jims and cheese packs in jars on the counter.

Kareem is like I was when I was little—always here at the store. But he don't just come for candy. He comes and tells me things. They found one of my grandfather's shoes, thanks to him. It was in a vacant building; cut wide open, toe to toe. Grown-ups in this neighborhood don't snitch. But little kids sometimes do. I never asked Kareem how he knew the shoe was there. He just told the police he was playing and he saw it. So anything he wants from me, he can have. I remember that and reach for the cookie jar.

Kareem is nine, and little for his age. He wobbles when he walks. My grandmother says he'll be a little person when he grows up. She's wrong. He's already a little person. He was born that way. Because he's little he overdoes everything, like driving his dad's car five miles once and crashing it. Or sneaking out the house one night, and ending up in the police station with some guys twice his age. Kareem is the one who gave me Melvin's name and address; the guy who almost cut me today. "Don't do me no more favors, Kareem. I almost got killed today because of you." I sit on a stool and tell him everything.

"I *thought* it was him," he says, finishing his cookie. "You sure he ain't do it?" He sits on my grandfather's stool and tells me that we're gonna find the right person for sure if we don't give up. Then he asks me to open the big jar on the counter.

"Pickled eggs never rot or nothing. They keep 'em in the store like for a year before they throw 'em out." His short, fat fingers go straight for the biggest, slipperiest egg. Then he tells me about the time he put six eggs in his mouth at once. Kareem makes things up sometimes. He lies, I guess you could say. But he's a kid, so I figure it's okay. And he wants to be big inside, my grandfather used to tell me. He would let him run the cash register, since the thing about Kareem is that he knows more about money than the people who run the numbers house six blocks away, I bet. And he knows everybody and all the streets around here, too.

I get to work, standing seven grocery bags in the middle of the floor and putting candy in them. Here's what I figure: I'll give some to Kareem and his sisters, then knock on doors and just give the rest away.

"What about Llee?" Kareem asks. "He wants some."

It's like Llee and Kareem planned it, because right then Llee shows up. "You giving stuff away today?" he asks.

I look at Kareem, then at Llee, who is seven and a half. Just like me and Kareem, he can't stay away from this store. "Where we gonna get candy now?" Kareem wants to know. Llee asks why they can't get candy here. Kareem explains. I keep working, taking down the frame on the wall with the first dollar bill my grandfather ever made. I'll put that in my room.

They eat and talk and try to change my mind. And then Llee says, "I know who killed Mr. Jenson."

He's said it before. I'm not falling for it again, especially after today. So I change the subject and bring up the Boy Scouts. I'm starting a troop for them this summer. A few minutes later, Llee and Kareem bring up the shooting again. It's always on their minds. There's something wrong with that, I think, little kids always talking about death.

Kareem starts talking about my grandfather's shoes.

"You think who killed him spent the money?" he asks.

Granddad wore penny loafers. There were nickels in them that my great-grandmother gave him when he was little. Those nickels were eighty-five years old. And he swore they were worth a thousand bucks each. That wasn't true, my grandmother said the day of his funeral. But he told everybody that story. Someone believed him. Otherwise we would have buried him in those shoes.

Llee sits on the floor, dumping candy between his legs, counting each piece twice. "I wasn't listening, but I heard," he says, chewing sticky candy, then scratching his front tooth like a lottery ticket, trying to get it off. "He said Pokei was mad at your grandfather because . . ."

"Who said?"

Llee's sucking red Kool-Aid from a straw, pouring the rest in his hand, licking it until it's gone. "Is my tongue red?"

"*Who* are you talking about, Llee?"

"Pokei." He crosses his eyes and stares at his tongue.

"Who's Pokei?" I change my mind. "Forget it, don't tell me."

"I don't know. My uncle just said Pokei did it."

I live in the suburbs, sixty miles from here. I only know the kids on this block, and a few a couple of blocks away. The older ones won't tell me anything. They say

I'm lame. Soft. And they're not getting killed for me. So I listen to Llee and Kareem, even though I should know better.

Kareem wants to know what kind of gun killed my grandfather. I used to know, but I forget. "Nobody's gonna shoot me," he says, aiming his finger at me. "'Cause I'm gonna get 'em first."

"Me too," Llee says. He points at me. "I want a rifle when I get your age. That's a big gun."

I wanted a Game Boy when I was his age. Kareem walks over and stands beside me. "If you had a gun, would you shoot him?"

"Shoot who?"

"Him." He's looking at my granddad's empty chair. "The man that took his shoes."

"My grandfather hated guns. He wouldn't want me doing something like that." That's what I'm saying, but that's not the whole truth. Lately I've been thinking if I got my hands on one . . . if I found out who did it . . . then they'd know how it felt. I don't ever let Llee and Kareem know what I'm really thinking, though, or how much I want to get even. "Let's talk about the Boy Scouts." I pull out my old belt, the one with over a hundred badges on it. "What's the first badge we're gonna work on? Let's see . . . there's cooking, sewing, babysitting." They both start talking at once, asking if I think they are girls or something. I ask them what Boy Scouts do.

"Hike."

"Help people."

"Camp."

They remember what I taught them.

"I been wanting to go camping since I was born," Llee says.

I sit down. Kareem is practically in my lap. "I went hiking once," he says. "But next time I wanna make a fire by myself, and eat marshmallows off a stick and tell scary stories." Then he asks if I'm sure the Scouts will give me a troop.

"Sure they will," I say, reminding myself to call and find out.

They chill out after a while, and help me pack bags. We even go outside and throw a few balls. But as soon as we get back inside, drinking orange soda and finishing off a bag of Hot Cheetos, Kareem whispers to Llee, "I know where Pokei lives."

My mouth is dry. My fingers won't stay away from my head, scratching my scalp so much you'd think I had lice. "Just finish filling up the bags."

"Do you think he cried?"

I look over at Llee.

"Do you think Grandpop Jenson cried when he got shot?"

I don't want to talk about this, so I ask them to leave. Only inside, way deep down inside, I hear a voice say, *If you don't find 'em, who will? If you don't handle your grandfather's business, who's gonna?*

They get quiet, and then Kareem asks me if I want him to take me to Pokei's place. That just makes me mad. "We don't even know if he even did it! And what if he did?" I say, taking a bag of good candy and dumping it in the trash can. "Who's gonna say he did? Nobody. Because nobody tells on nobody around here, even when they kill a nice old man who gave candy away for free."

Kareem knows when to back off, so he changes the subject. "What color uniform we gonna wear? Where we gonna meet?"

I'm thinking about Pokei now, not the Scouts. I go and sit down by Llee. "Is your uncle the only one saying Pokei did it, or did you hear it somewhere else too?"

He puts up two fingers like a Scout. I taught him that. "Everybody's saying it."

Kareem digs down to the bottom of the egg jar. "If Mr. Jenson had a gun, he wouldn't be dead. Pokei would be dead. And the store wouldn't be closing."

"*Bang. Pop. Pop. Pop.* Pokei's dead now, good." Llee's

got one knee on the ground, and a finger aimed at Kareem, who stands up and fires back.

I slap his trigger finger. "Quit it," I say, "and go home. I have to fix my grandmother lunch." I don't, but my stomach is a little queasy. That happens sometimes when I talk about this stuff too long. I'm wondering about Pokei, though. What if he is the one? What if he cashed in the nickel and still has the shoe?

"I can take you to his house," Kareem says. "Right now if you wanna."

Kareem isn't always wrong. Llee either. Once my grandmother lost her purse and they took her to the house of the kid who found it. The money was gone, but not the credit cards. "You two need to leave," I say, picking up two big bags. "Come on, Llee, you're first." I walk out the door. Llee's right behind me. If I go to Pokei's place, I'll take something with me, I think. Gotta protect myself.

Llee and Kareem live on opposite ends of the block, and neither one of them has brothers, so I don't mind looking out for them. Llee hugs me when I drop him off, and asks if I'll take them to the basketball court later. "Sure," I say, heading back to the store.

When I come back for Kareem, I ask for Pokei's address, just in case. Then I pick up two bags and start walking him up the street. Kareem's older sister, Sahara, answers the door and asks if I'm nuts, giving him so much junk food. "You know he hyper," she says, telling him to put that candy away until their mom gets home.

I'm halfway up the street when I hear Kareem yelling my name. "Take this," he says catching up to me. The brown paper bag is wrinkled and greasy. "My father work at a garage and people leave stuff. You can have it 'cause you gave me all that candy."

"What is it?"

He sits on the curb, opening the bag like it's lunch he's not sure he wants to eat. Out comes bunches of old newspaper. Kareem tells me to look in the bag. He's smiling. Proud of himself.

I've never seen a real gun before.

Kareem stares up at me. "One time Mr. Jenson bought me a coat. He said mine was too small. I still got it." He stares into the bag, reaching inside.

I stop him. "Don't do that."

Kareem is like Llee. He'll do what I say. So he sits with his hands in his lap. "My father forgets about it," he says. "But sometime I go outside . . . and practice." He unties a shoelace.

"You do what?"

He asks me not to tell, then says how sometimes he sneaks out while his parents are working and pretends to shoot the trees. "But one day I'm gonna do it for real."

"Shoot trees?"

"Shoot something. Something . . . big."

My fingers can't tie his laces without shaking. "You have to put it back, Kareem."

"But Pokei shot Mr. Jenson."

"You don't know that."

"Maybe he ain't do it. But I bet he knows who did."

Since I came here last month I've been wanting whoever took out my grandfather to be dead too. Getting even, that's what's been on my mind; in my dreams. I can't talk to my parents about it. They'd say nice boys don't think that way. I can't tell my grandmother because she's got her own problems. My uncles are lawyers—two of them, anyhow. If I say something like this to them, they'll tell me that the law gets even for people. Only Llee and Kareem know what I think. They know what I want, what we all want: for someone to do what the police can't or won't. I swallow. I tell myself that people like me don't do stuff like this. But I ask for the bullets anyhow. "How do you put them in?"

He wants to show me. "Just tell me," I say.

His father goes hunting, and takes him sometimes. He showed him how to load and unload last year. Kareem shot a possum, a raccoon, and three mice—nothing human, he tells me. But he's ready to, he says.

I dig down deep until I feel metal. The barrel. The neck. The handle. Then I grab the bag and start running. Kareem follows, like usual.

We run up the street and into the store, locking the garage door behind us. The bag goes on the counter. We sit on stools, staring at it. It's real, that gun. "And it kills," I say, watching my fingers shake. I look inside. When I pick it up it feels like it's mine already. I relax a little.

"You can do it," Kareem whispers.

"Huh?"

"They do it all the time on TV; around here, too." He's got his fingers in the egg jar again. "I ain't scared of nobody . . . nothing. So when I'm your age and somebody mess with me, they gone." He pulls his dripping wet hand out of the jar and turns it into a gun. "Let me show you how to do it." Pink water drips on the stool like blood.

"Do what?" I say.

"Show you how to kill."

I sit myself down—so I don't fall down. Kareem keeps talking, asking if I think my grandfather's in heaven. Before I answer, he's on to Llee. "I let him hold it once."

I look at him.

"Llee's afraid of guns. But he ain't gonna be soon."

Everything stops—the hum from the cooler, the water dripping from Kareem's fingers, even the ant sneaking across the floor. I think about Llee and Kareem all by themselves with guns and nobody to stop 'em from shooting each other.

Kareem can't keep quiet. He's been thinking, he says, asking me to promise not to tell nobody what he's about to tell me. But before I can promise, he's talking. His father's gun spent the night with Llee one time. "By accident. I forgot it. We play with it over there sometimes, but don't nobody know. I'm the cowboy . . . 'cause it's mine."

All of a sudden, my bowels get so loose so fast I almost don't make it to the bathroom. I'm in there so long, Kareem knocks on the door three times, asking what's wrong.

By the time I finish and figure out what to do, Kareem is done eating half a box of donuts. I sit at the counter with him, telling him to wipe his mouth. I stare at the gun, and then at the frame with the dollar in it. I ask Kareem if he wants it. I don't know why. Then I hand it to him. "He never hurt anyone, Kareem."

"I know. That's what I like about him. He was nice."

I wrap the gun up in brown paper, like sausage, and put it in the bag. I do the same with the frame, making sure Kareem understands that he's got to take care of it. "Let's go," I tell him.

He jumps down and follows me. He knows a shortcut

to Pokei's place, he says. But he thinks we should check out the jitney station first. "He be there day and night."

I'm locking the door, looking at the stuff over by the curb. Yesterday somebody put new shoes there. "So you can walk all over heaven, Mr. J," a note says.

We stop in front of Westina's house. She worked at the store too. Then we pass the twins' house. They're in college. My grandfather would send them each twenty bucks a month. Llee's house is next. Then Kareem's. He passes it by, though, and doesn't look back until he's almost at the corner. By then I'm up his steps and ringing the bell.

"No!"

He runs back to the house, pulling at the bag while I lean on his doorbell again and again.

"Give me that."

I hold it high over his head.

"I'll put it back. Promise."

He jumps up and down, grabbing for it. "Don't get me in trouble."

My feet get stepped on. My legs get pushed. I don't budge.

Kareem is a little kid, and all little kids cry when they know they're about to get in trouble. So does he. "I won't do it no more," he says, hanging on to my legs, begging.

I hand his dad the bag. "Kareem gave me this."

I hear Kareem just as clear as I hear my grandfather sometimes tell me to take care of things while he's gone. "Snitch," he says.

His father opens the bag and looks at me. He stares at Kareem, pulling him inside with one hand. "Thanks," he says to me. "His mother been sayin' we need to get him some help. Guess we better."

I head for the store. Summer won't be the same now. Everything's messed up. Kareem might not even want to join the Scouts. And Llee, what'll he do if he's not at the store, bugging me?

I open the store door, then close it right back. Before I know it I'm walking up the steps of my grandparents' house. I sit on the swing, thinking of ways to get my grandmother to change her mind. People need this store— I do too—even if it's not a real store; just a garage full of candy. Besides, can't nobody fill my grandfather's shoes but me. And can't nobody talk to Kareem and Llee about getting over getting even but me, either. Otherwise we'll all be trying to get even until the day we die. And Granddad would say that's a stupid way to live.

PEOPLE MIGHT NOT UNDERSTAND

When I'm president of the world,
I'll move the White House to Harlem,
Outlaw guns—especially the ones they make
    to take out you and me.
When I'm president of the world,
Babies won't ever go hungry,
Pampers and cable TV will be free,
And houses in the hood will look like the ones on
    HGTV.
I'll fix the hole in the ozone,
Make it illegal to be grown and styling in the same
    clothes that your kids put on.
When I'm president of the world,
I will listen more than talk,
Walk
    instead of ride.

That way I'll see America through other people's eyes.
When I am president of the world,
I will still come for dinner on Sundays.
But no chicken, please.
People might not understand.

FAKIN' IT

IF YOUR AUNTIE WAKES YOU UP at four in the morning, telling you to get the heck on outta her crib now, you got the right to knock her upside the head—*pow!* Only I ain't that kind of dude. I got respect. Even though this little voice in my head says to clock this broad, I turn around, face the wall, and shut my eyes. "Awright, Aunt Philomena," I say, pulling blankets over my head. "Get on up outta here."

She's short, with legs as skinny as the branches on the artificial tree by the window in the basement. But she thinks she's tough. So she don't back down. She grabs the covers with both hands and pulls. I have to hold on to the window ledge not to get drug off, too. Me kicking her arms slows her down, but it don't stop her. She pulls my right arm. I snatch it back. She grabs my left foot. I use my other one to get her off me. Then I take back what's mine—the Cleveland Browns blanket she bought for me last Christmas.

Out of breath, breathing hard like she needs that ventilator her friend uses when she comes visiting, Auntie leans against the wall. "God, God . . ."

She is always talking about God.

"God gave you ears, didn't he? Then get up . . . get out of here," she says, holding her chest.

I'm yelling too. "This is my room! You get out!" It's hot underneath the covers; in the house, too. She's sixty-three, with arthritis in her joints, so it's always a thousand degrees in here. But I stay covered up anyhow, tucking my feet under the blanket and using my fists to hold down the other ends. "Stop pulling!" I curse at her. I have to.

"You cursing me, boy? You swearing . . . in my house?" Auntie pulls and my hammertoe feels air. But she ain't no dude, I'm stronger than her, so after my head is free and I'm breathing in deep, I reach back and jerk the covers again. She flies into bed with me this time, smacking my forehead, then my lips—aiming for my head. "What I say? What did I say? Get out!"

I warn her for the last time. "Just because you my auntie don't mean I won't hit you," I say, pulling back the covers.

"You did everything else that you could do to

me. Hitting was probably next on the list anyhow."

For one whole minute she and me just stare at each other, neither one of us blinking. Ain't no hug coming from her this time. Ain't no apology finding its way to my lips, like it sometimes do. It's over, living here with her. No turning back now.

"Screw you." I come out from underneath the covers. The sheets, too. Then I'm on my feet, heading for my dresser, showing her what I been trying not to show her all this time.

She stands up, her eyes squeezed closed. "Boy! I ain't your mother—cover up."

Auntie Philomena is the crazy one. The one everyone warned me about when my father kicked me out and told me to go live someplace else—anyplace as long as it wasn't in his house, his city, his state. Auntie heard about that. She called me and asked if I wanted to come live with her. "Just you and me, baby." Five bedrooms, two baths, and a pool. "What'll say?" Of course I said yeah. Otherwise I'd be homeless. No one else wanted me. And I never had my own room or a pool to swim in before—which is what I've done every day since I came here a year ago. Now this nutcase is kicking me out, like she and me ain't family. "Listen," I say, pushing her so hard her head knocks against my bedroom door. "I didn't ask to come here. You asked me." I open and close drawers, throwing new shirts on the floor, stepping on them like they rags our dog, Malcolm, sleeps on sometimes.

She swears if I don't put something on and pick up them good shirts she bought, she'll wring my neck. I take my time stepping into a clean pair of undies that I ironed myself. "I was doing you a favor, coming here." I sit on the side of the bed, checking out the bags under her eyes. They so black and heavy she puts cucumbers on 'em sometimes. "Who wants to live with you anyhow?" I point to her belly that always looks pregnant. It was my job, she said, to make sure she ain't eat after eight p.m. To keep her hands off the chocolate milk and out the cookie jar. "Get stanky fat," I say. "See if I care."

She sits, staring out the window, not trying to explain why she putting me out.

"What I do?" I want to ask. But I don't. I walk into my closet and come back with suitcases. Then turn on the fan to cool us both off.

I am always packing; always leaving someplace. So it don't matter, leaving her too. It's just this time I didn't see it coming. I screwed up; forgot myself. Thought this was really home. That won't happen no more.

Auntie keeps her eyes on me. "I know how to pack," I say. "You don't have to watch."

She is stubborn. Everyone in our family is. So she just sits, ignoring Malcolm when he walks in and lies by her feet. Ignoring me too when I say for the ninetieth time for her to leave. She's so talkative usually. This morning her lips are sealed, except to tell me what I need to do to be out in the next two hours.

"Fake." The word comes out long and slow. I wanna make sure she hears me, so I say it again. "Fake." It's like a smack to the face. It makes her hold her cheek, then wipe her lips with the back of her hand.

Auntie pats her head, checking for rollers that fall out like her hair sometimes does. Then she's out of the chair; hot as red peppers. "I'm just as good as they are! A lottery winner's money spends as good as a doctor's money do."

Once I told her she was fake for living in this neighborhood like she some kind of executive, or a doctor, like the woman from Pakistan who lives up the street and got a lawn as big as the new kiddie park the city built. But that's not what I'm talking about now. I say it again, looking at her the way the man up the street looked at me once—like I was lower than the slug holes I find in the lawns sometimes. "You a fake. The biggest one ever."

She picks at the eczema on her hands and the side of her face. Sometimes it was me that put medicine on it. "I know they talk about me," she says, scratching too hard.

"I know they think I don't belong up here." She's quiet for a while. Thinking about *them*, I guess. "But I earned the right to be here."

"So did I."

Auntie was the one who said there was nothing I could ever do to get kicked out of her house. That was one whole year ago, the longest time I've ever stayed with anyone except my dad. I thought it was forever, her and me. But grown-ups change the rules when they want.

I go to the closet, take out more pants. I shut her up, for a little while anyhow. She hates when I talk about her living in this neighborhood. She wants to fit in. She never will. Me either, I guess.

Auntie points to the attic. "You got more suitcases up there." She bought them before I got here; before she drove me across three states, showing me places I never seen or heard of before. I look at the Statue of Liberty she bought for me. And pack it. Then sit it back on the dresser that I dusted yesterday. "Why don't you just get out?" The plastic statue hits the wall and breaks.

I got a temper. She's got a temper. When we both get angry, it's like World War Ten up in here. One day after we finished arguing and making up, we watched a television show on Greek gods. For a while she called me Zeus—the god of love and thunder. I'm never gonna forget that, 'cause it was like she was comparing me to someone important; powerful, too. And when I hooked up with my crew, that's the name I took—Zeus—'cause when I'm pissed I spit fire, and when somebody do me wrong I'll destroy 'em, one way or the other.

"I just . . . need to be by myself doing this," I say, feeling tired from getting up so early.

Sometimes Auntie listens. She gets out of the chair. Tells Malcolm to come and eat, and leaves me alone. I keep packing, thinking, wondering. Where to next? I'm running out of relatives. My father has three other sisters who pretend to care about me too. They send cards on my birthday. They always have. And they call every few months or so. But they don't want me living with them. No one does.

I lock my door. I sit on the bed. And think about what I did. Nothing. I didn't do nothing. She's just old. Mean. Fronting.

When one suitcase is filled, I start on another one. Open more drawers; stare inside. My shirts and sweaters are perfect—sitting in my drawers the way they sit on department store shelves. I'm good like that. She never had to tell me to vacuum or clean up—I did it just for fun. I clean like a thousand-dollar-an-hour maid, my father always said. But I can fire you up like Zeus.

This is real. The words come into my head like a warning. *You gotta leave. And you don't have nowhere else to go.*

"Shoot." I pat my pockets, check underneath my bed for my cell. Then I remember. "Dag." She took it last week. I was on punishment and she grabbed it while I was in the shower. When my punishment was over, she said Malcolm got to it. It looked like a hammer smashed it; not like a shepherd chewed it up. But she said she'd buy me a new one this week. "All that time, you was lying to me!" I shout. Sitting down, holding my stomach, feeling sick. We talked and laughed and joked around. And all that time she was planning to kick me out.

"Think. Think. Think," I tell myself. But all my numbers were in my phone. She stepped on it once before— right in front of me. "Because of them," she said. "Bad influences." She's putting me out because of them too, I guess.

I open the door and lean over the hallway railing. "You crazy, you know that?"

She keeps singing about Jesus. Auntie ain't never been married. Who would want to marry her? Big mouth. Know-it-all. Think she's hard. Think she's blessed 'cause she hit the big one for six million. Man. I seen her bank account. I've watched her writing checks to that stupid church and putting money aside for my college education when I don't even want to go to college. "Your mother would want you to." She always said that.

My mother left when I was three. For four years they told me she had died. But she wasn't dead, just gone. By the time my father decided to tell the truth, she was living in Nevada, married to a man from Jamaica who had two kids before he gave her three more. She asked if I wanted to come and live with her. For what? That's what I tell her when she calls twice a year. If she wanted me, she would have taken me with her. But she left me with him. And he never liked me. Maybe that ain't true. Never got me; understood me. That's it. He was ex-military, a workaholic who stayed gone more than he stayed at home, so by the time he knew anything, I was twelve and a half and had my own way of thinking and doing things. Military dudes only know how to do things one way—their way. So I skipped school, stayed out whenever I wanted, and got to liking blunts and the taste of gin—straight up. He couldn't make me do what he wanted, and the cops couldn't either. So he said I had to leave. I tried living with my mother for a while. But it turns out I ain't like her much either. Then there was Auntie Marcella and Auntie Champagne. The uncles on my mother's side all passed on me. They said I'd make 'em hurt me. I lived with Aunt Chrystal on my mother's side for three days. But she said if I didn't get out right that minute, she was turning me in to the police. My dad picked me up and kept me for twenty-four hours. I got here, I guess, by way of my father's baby sister, whose house I ended up at next. The family had a conference call about me. Auntie Philomena was on the line, saying she'd come for me. They warned her not to. They said foster care or a group home might be just what I needed. In the middle of the night, Aunt Philomena showed up anyhow. She had to drive all night. But she did it. "'Cause family do that kind of thing," she said.

I changed—tried to anyhow, once I came to live here. I didn't sport no colors. I didn't go to the mall unless it was her and me. I never asked to go to the neighborhoods that kids like me live in. I stayed in the house. I didn't mind the quiet or the stares or that time someone called the cops 'cause they didn't know I lived around here.

I tried so hard to do good; to do right. But high school ain't nice like they always portraying it on TV. It's hardcore. Scary. Even here in the burbs. The school was so white. And the teachers and classes were so different. I been behind since first grade. Ninth grade just means I'm plain lost. So they might as well be speaking Portuguese at that school.

Cutting class is easy for me. Hitching a ride is like breathing: I do it all the time. Besides, they live in every city, in every town, on just about every block, I bet. Here wasn't no different. So one day, it happened. They found me. Or maybe I found them. You have to have somebody, even if you don't want to, I guess.

"Auntie." I open the door. Close it. I can't ask her to let me stay. She'd just say no. But I don't have no place else to go. I open the door wider. "I'm not going to live with her." I throw the words into the hall. They fall down the steps and she catches them.

"You go where I send you. Or get locked up—which is most likely to happen anyway."

I slam the door, almost catching Malcolm's tail when he walks in. "I'm not living with her." I kick hangers out my way. Pick up the lamp she bought at Macy's on sale for a hundred fifty bucks and aim it at the wall. If I could remember one phone number, get to just one of them.

I put it down. Sit back on my bed. Try as hard as I can to remember a number. Only I can't. It wouldn't matter anyway. I owe a few of 'em money. And they want it. Auntie told me she was gonna open an account for me. "Putting five thousand bucks in it for starters." She wanted me to learn to manage money. Big money. "'Cause one day it's all gonna be yours anyhow."

I pick up the picture frames, wrapping them in between my shorts and shirts. Leaving the one with her and me dressed in cowboy clothes right where it is. But I take the one we took at the mall. It was after church. We was eating someplace special. One of my boys saw us in the window and came in to say hello. Auntie doesn't understand. My boys are not like me. Old people are just old people to them—nothing special. So when she gave him a piece of her mind, like she was packing or something, he told me about it later. Said he would hurt her, and still might. "'Cause you gonna get the money anyhow, so why should we wait?"

I think that's why they lent to me. Why they let the debt build up so high. "I'm good for it," I always said, when I lost at craps.

"Malcolm, come." I let him get in my bed. Then I lay across it, too, patting him. Remembering how Auntie would come and find me when I stayed out too late, or all night long, even. I don't know how she did it, but she'd show up wherever I was. She'd tell my boys to keep quiet and for me to come home. Not leave when they'd say she'd better get gone or else. She grew up with six brothers. Two got killed in the war. One died of lung cancer and two more was shot on the street. "Bad boys run in our family like cancer," she'd say to them. "Dying don't scare me, so don't mess with me."

I couldn't figure out if they was joking or not when

they'd say, "Let's just off her. Tie her up. Burn her up. Get all that dough."

But I would always tell 'em straight up, "No. She my auntie. Y'all nuts?"

Now I'm here wishing I'd listened to them. The money. The house. It would all be mine.

I go to the bathroom and turn on the shower. Tiptoe up the hall and listen for Auntie, who is downstairs frying bacon and praising God. Her bedroom door creaks when I push it open. Perfume and pink are everywhere. I open the closet door slow so the creak don't give me away. The crystal clock on her dresser says I'd better hurry. The first drawer I open says I'm wasting my time. Her jewelry box plays music, so I stay away from it. The drawers with underwear and shirts, stockings and scarves don't even have any change in them.

"Jeffrey!"

She's at the bottom of the stairs, so I can't answer or she'll know where I am.

"You gonna miss that plane if we don't get moving."

She makes the best bacon. Coffee too. It's like her, I'm thinking, to give me a last meal—like they give prisoners in jail before they kill 'em.

I go into the third bedroom. Once I found a hundred bucks in a drawer. Nothing this time. Her emergency money ain't here. She's gonna make me leave broke. That's like her, too.

"Jeffrey!"

I lean over the railing. "Okay. I'm coming."

I take a quick shower, then get dressed and take one last look at my room. I never had one so nice; so big. I picked out the furniture. Painted the room myself. Got the most expensive bedding in the store, just about.

I sit, trying to get myself together, wondering why I can't never seem to get it right.

The front door downstairs opens. Auntie's speaking to a woman across the street, the jogger who starts out in the dark and is home before most people have their breakfast. Neighbors here ain't like the ones where I come from. They talk too much. Tell everything they see—me and my boys out front having a little smoke; me and my boys sitting 'round back on my own property drinking a forty, which ain't nobody's business but ours. Next thing I know Auntie knows about it. And I'm on restriction and my boys can't come visit, which is crazy because I am sixteen not six.

Did someone snitch? Did they say I was there with my boys when that thing with that kid went down?

Auntie talks to her about the weather. She asks how her husband's business is going. She mentions how the gardener is killing our trees and how she is going to Savannah in a few weeks—which she never told me.

It don't make sense, but I lay back down underneath the covers, thinking about her. How she always tried to make me something I wasn't. At home, my dad and I drank soda out the can. Auntie said people don't do things like that 'round here. I didn't like it at first, pouring root beer into a glass every time I drank one. But I got used to it. And after a while I didn't even mind not watching television while we ate. Sitting in the dining room was cool too. I never told my boys about the cloth napkins on my lap, or how she once had a friend of hers teach us how to set a proper table and which forks to use. Watching *The Simpsons* and *South Park* was a no-no. And BET was out of the question. Those were Auntie's rules. I followed 'em, too. My mother . . . my mother is different. At her place in Arizona I will be sleeping with three little boys—like before. And trouble will follow me like hot air.

I ask myself again, how did I blow this? What did I do?

The door shuts. Auntie's yelling up the stairs for me to come on. "Now."

But I'm not leaving. Not going empty-handed; broke. And she won't just give me the money, so . . . "I'm coming," I say, sitting my suitcases outside the door and locking Malcolm inside my room.

I take my time walking down the steps with them suitcases. Going back up and coming down with more.

"Jeffrey. Don't miss that plane, boy."

She's out the door and clearing more things from her car. I pick up a biscuit filled with bacon, eggs, and cheese and chew and swallow it quick. I down the glass of strawberry milk Auntie left sitting out for me. Then I pick up a knife. It caught my eye sitting in the silverware drawer with cake icing still stuck to it. I'm thinking I might need it.

She yells from outside for me to get myself moving.

It wasn't there when I first came downstairs. Or maybe it was and I didn't notice. But on my way to the powder room, I see the chain with the medallion she gave me, sitting on the dining room table. It's real gold. She paid seven hundred and sixty bucks for it, on sale. *Great Men Look Like You*, it says on the back.

It's in my right hand. The knife's in my left hand when Auntie walks up behind me. I hold on to my medallion, feeling it dig into my palm. The chain broke three months ago. I asked her to get it fixed a million times. It's like her, to have it all perfect now. She backs up when she sees the knife.

I wait for her to go nuts. She's waiting for me to make a move.

My fingers squeeze the knife hard.

She says I already broke her heart so I might as well stab her in it too.

Auntie's old, but her back's straight. She's scared, I bet, but she'd never show it. So we stand there. Me, Zeus. Her, Hestia—goddess of goddesses. Her finger shakes when she reaches for my lips and wipes crumbs off. Then she pats my cheek and says, "It shoulda worked out."

She and me was good for each other, most times anyway. Maybe if I ask to stay. Tell her it will be different this time, she might change her mind.

I throw the knife into the corkboard behind the kitchen sink. It sticks. Her fingers find more crumbs. "Auntie . . . can I . . . sta—"

"No more chances," she tells me. Then she asks why I can't do right. Why don't I want to be good?

She ruins everything with that big mouth of hers. The next thing I know, I've got suitcases in my hands and I'm walking out the door.

I climb into the backseat. Auntie gets behind the wheel. She looks nervous, talks a little too loud about the weather. "Wait a minute," she says, getting out the car and going back inside. When she comes back, there's a baseball bat in her hand. She puts the car in reverse and pulls into the street. The sign says stop; she keeps rolling. It might as well say do whatever you want. She flies through two more stop signs anyhow.

We pass the lawns that I mowed and the houses where people gave me iced tea or lemonade to fight the heat. Before we leave the complex, I look at the medallion again. *"Great Men Look Like You."* I read it out loud and sit back. She smiles, and relaxes a little.

But not for long.

Her eyes bug when she sees my colors. My eyes dare her to say something, anything, 'cause this is just the way things are. Doing right comes out wrong no matter where I go. And grown-ups get just as tired as I do of trying to make things work. But when I get to wherever I'm going, I don't have to be all by myself. They'll be there. Not my father. Not her. Them—my crew.

I finish tying up my head, checking out my colors in her mirror, laughing at the look on her face. Then I sit back, feeling taller, stronger than I have all morning.

The chain breaks when I try to put it around my neck. The medallion hits my knee, then jumps under her seat, like it wants to get away from me too. "Fake," I say, sending the chain after it; leaning back and wondering where to next.

DYING BEFORE I'M DONE

In case somebody shoots me,
In case someone does me in,
Here's what you should know about me.
I am a loyal, dependable friend.
I eat ice cream with a fork.
I love bacon, but I'm allergic to pork.
Cookies with sprinkles are my favorite treat.
I know it's gross, but I like to smell my own feet.
In sixth grade I made all A's,
By eighth grade I was more into babes.
There's a secret only my mother knows.
Every Mother's Day I polish her toes.
There are lots of things I plan to do.
Spend a summer working at the Louvre,
Take my sister to New York on the train,
Convince my dad to ride in an airplane,

Show my brother how to have a good time playing
    chess instead of drinking wine.
Only some things end sooner than you want,
Like your first kiss and fourth-period lunch.
So if I die before I'm done,
Don't let 'em forget
While I was here, I had me some fun.

SIXTEEN

My ride
My boys
My game
My girl
My world.

FAT MAN WALKING

He STOPS, SO I STOP.

Sweat is running down the left side of his face. The front of his shirt is soaked and we've only walked two blocks. I hold on to his arm. It's hot, like the sun is trapped inside him. "You okay?"

He's leaning on a parking meter. It looks so small standing beside him. Like a celery stick next to a watermelon.

A car stops at the light. The window rolls down.

"They staring," I say to my father.

"I know."

"I hate that."

"Let's keep walking," he says, not moving. "They ignorant, that's all."

Everyone in that car starts laughing. Before I know it, a stone has left my hand and is headed for the guy who's asking my dad if he wants his empty pizza box—"Because I can see you don't waste a thing when you eat."

The stone hits the car. Dad tries to stop me from picking up more. "Harvey, quit it."

It's too late. The stone hit the hood and the windshield, too. The driver is out of his car, asking if I wanna get hurt this morning. "'Cause the last person who touched my ride is six feet under."

"Stop making fun of my father."

Pops apologizes to the driver, then says, "An eleven-and-a-half-year-old shrimp who loves his daddy. What can I do?" He's got his arm over my shoulder, his sweaty rolls sticking to my neck. Then he smiles. "No harm done, right?"

The guy doesn't mind holding up traffic while he rubs the top of his car with a dry cloth. "I'm just saying . . . you better tell him . . . somebody gonna hurt him . . . and I don't mind it being me."

We start walking, with me staring back over my shoulder at that guy, just in case. We don't get far, only a few steps. "Now, Harvey, you've got . . . you can't. . . . Lord," Pops, says, trying to catch his breath, "it sure is hot."

"Sure is."

He pats his stomach with both hands. I lean on the black Jeep parked at the curb. He holds on to another meter. Pops weighs so much—five-twenty last time he hit the scale—that even walking twenty steps can take his breath away. We couldn't find a parking space close to the store because of all the construction, and everyone out here shopping for back-to-school stuff. Today will be doubly worse for me, because my friends will all be out here. They know Dad is fat. But they don't hardly ever see him walking, except from the door to the front porch, or from the living room to the kitchen. So when they do see him out, their eyes bug. Their words are respectful, but you can see what they think on their faces: *Dag, your pops is big. Man, what a whopper. Wow, Harvey, glad he ain't my dad.*

We walk half a block. The back of his shirt is wet now too. "We can go back home. The car's not that far away," I say.

He wipes his neck and forehead dry. "All summer we been sacrificing for these, right?" He pats his pocket, the one with the coupon in it. The sneakers are on sale. Everyone's gonna have 'em when school starts in two weeks. Me too, now. They still cost a hundred eighty bucks, but Dad said he'd do what he had to do to make sure I got 'em. And he did. He didn't buy no Pepsi all summer. Hardly ever put the air conditioner on either. And he did something I figured no man would ever do—take in laundry. "Ain't no Laundromat around here. People take a jitney or bus to get to one. Then they pay three-fifty to wash, and almost that to dry." He was saving them money, and making some too.

We have an extra-large washer and dryer because of him. He bought 'em two years ago when he gained so much he couldn't leave the house. Then he went on a diet with Oprah and lost weight. Then he gained seventy-five pounds back. He can't go to work no more. And disability doesn't pay enough. I told him not to do other people's clothes. He was already writing out Miss Naomi's bills— she's blind. And he was already tutoring the Simons' kids in math and teaching Jonquil Miller how to play piano. But laundry? Naw. Only after I got into six fights over kids teasing me about it, it didn't bother me that much. I won most of the time. And they shut up, especially after I started telling people about Ray Ray's drawers always having brown streaks up the middle; Parole's mom's bras being so yellow that bleach can't clean 'em; and Washington's pop's shirts being smeared with pink lipstick, on the collar and on his undershirts, too.

Dad's walking and sweating again. Me too. "Want something to drink?" I'm looking at the blue water cooler out front of Bernie's Bistro. Bottles stick up out of crushed ice, sweaty cold. "I'll pay," I tell Dad. Before he can say anything, I'm pulling out three bucks and screwing off the tops and watching him lean against a car and gulp down the water, still half frozen in the bottle. A lady cuts her eyes at him, 'cause the left side of the car is leaning close to the ground.

He smacks his lips. "Now that's good. Ready?"

"Ready."

He's limping by the time we get to the end of the block. It's that left foot, I bet. The one that had pressure sores on it all last year, big sores that ooze pus. I think they're back. He looks embarrassed. "Walking with me is like walking to Mars, huh? Take you forever to get where you going."

"It's too hot to move fast." I point across the street to a guy on Rollerblades flying past everyone. "Even if I had on skates, I'd be walking." I pull out a handkerchief and wipe my face, then hand it to him—his own is too wet to use now. "Even skating makes you sweat in this weather."

Pops wipes my forehead. "Skates are next. I haven't forgot what I promised you."

"It's okay. School's starting soon; snow will be coming next. Can't skate on that." I walk backward, closing one eye to block the sun, keeping the other on him.

Dixon Street isn't steep, but you'd think it was if you heard my father breathing. I said we didn't have to come today. Besides the heat, it's Saturday—the worst day to be on the avenue. But he said he was coming even if I didn't.

That's how he is. Sometimes my friends ask if I like being adopted. Being adopted by him is the best, I tell them. Only I worry that something might happen to him one day.

When my dad asks me for the time, I tell him I don't know. It'll just upset him, knowing how long we've been at this. It'll be an hour and a half by the time we get there. Anyhow, what can he do? Lose weight? It just comes back like shingles. The lady next door has 'em, and she says they never go away for good.

"I'm sorry." He leans on me this time, looking a little sick. "Shouldn'ta tried to do all this walking today." Sweat runs over his forehead and into his eyes. He wipes it off his wet ears too. I pull up the back of his shirt.

"Don't . . . !"

I fan to give him a breeze.

"Boy, you something," he says, reaching back and patting my arm. "That sure feels good."

We take a few more steps and he frowns, closes his eyes tight, biting his bottom lip.

"Is it your legs, Dad?" They cramp sometimes. I rub them for him at night. Wrap 'em in hot rags, too. "I'll take care of 'em when we get back home."

"Man, oh man. I'll be glad when I'm your size again." He laughs, rubbing the back of my head. "Maybe we should get something to eat. What do you say?"

We see a guy at Leo's Pizzeria throwing dough in the air and catching it. Pans of pizza sit in the window—chicken, pepperoni, sausage, veggie, pineapple. Pops wants to go in. Not me. He doesn't need it. But I *am* hungry, and he needs to rest. Before I say okay, two women start to pass by us. The closest one sniffs, then leans his way and sniffs again. Dad pretends not to notice, but I do. And I know it's not the pizza she's sniffing. It happens whenever we go out—someone's just got to know if he stinks, 'cause naturally all fat people stink, don't they?

"Ready, Dad?"

He smiles at them. "Hey, ladies."

I hate when he speaks to people who are rude to him.

"Hot day, isn't it?"

They give him fake smiles. And the one in the orange dress moves closer to her friend, like fat is contagious. "Too hot," she says, sniffing then stopping in the middle of the pavement, fanning herself.

I can't hit girls or women. That's a house rule. But I wish I could, because sometimes they deserve it, especially when it comes to Pops.

Pops pats his left leg. I know what that means. He's gotta sit down or he'll fall down. "We have to go," I say, almost pushing the one in purple out the way.

She looks down her nose at me and takes another whiff.

"We're trying to find Eileen's. A hairdresser shop." She turns her head and sneezes. "Sinuses." She blows into a Kleenex. "Pollen," she and my dad both say. Then she's blowing, rubbing her nose like someone put itching power up it.

Sometimes people surprise me. She looked just the type to stick her nose in his business and tell him about a diet or some pill she heard works really well on super fat people. Dad and I say we don't know nothing about Eileen's. He jokes about his hair needing to be done, though. He doesn't have any, so the women both laugh.

"Ready?" He asks me this time.

"Sure."

Some doorways are small, like the one at Leo's. So if you are too big, you have to kind of walk in a little sideways. I look straight ahead when he does that, because people are staring. They always do.

Pops takes the first seat he gets. Naturally it's made for a skinny guy. It's like me trying to sit on the tip of a pencil. I jump up. "I'ma ask them where the big chairs are."

Pops says the seat's just fine. "An incentive for me to lose weight."

I sit down and ask what he wants to eat. The guy looks over at Dad when I order two slices of pepperoni, thin crust. "That's it? You sure?"

"And two drinks—extra large."

No one would believe it, but my pops takes forever to eat. So we are sitting there for twenty-five minutes. His one slice turns into two, though. Mine turns into three. "After the shoes, what next?" he asks, wiping sauce off of my chin.

I say we can go back home, but I don't really mean it. We hardly ever get to the avenue anymore. It's too hard on my pops. He doesn't even drive all that much—the steering wheel hurts his stomach. So I take the bus to the grocery store. And I drop off bill payments sometimes, too. I don't mind. Pops and I do stuff like that for each other.

"We're out," he says, patting his foot. "Let's stay out."

"There it is!"

We both stop and stare. The Sneaker People is about twelve stores up. People are walking in like the store is giving away free food with each pair of sneakers. "You got the coupon, right?"

Pops nods. It's the second time I asked him that in the last few minutes. "Hey." He stops again, to catch his breath, I figure. "Isn't that Willie over there?"

Willie crosses the street, yelling my name at the same time. When he gets to us, he and I talk about the sneakers we're getting. We want the same kind. "Let's go. They're buying 'em all up. Jabril texted me." He's walking too fast. And he wants me to hurry up. I can't. I got Pops.

"Go ahead," Dad says.

"Naw. That's okay."

"I didn't even wait for my mother," Willie says, turning back to us. "It's taking her too long to park."

Pops says it again. "Go on. I'm right behind you."

People are walking out the store with two and three boxes. And Willie won't wait. "See y'all," he says, taking off.

I look at Pops. "I won't try 'em on until you get there," I say. And then I take off after Willie.

So many sneakers. That's all I think when I walk into the store. So many people, too. I look around for a seat for Pops. "Here they are." Willie puts one in my hand. And for a while that's all I can think about—the sneakers everybody wants. The most expensive ones I've ever owned.

The salesmen are busy. We can't get their attention. Willie checks out more sneakers. I hold on to the one I got. Three boys from our school come in. I look at the door for Pops. But then we get to talking, trying on sunglasses and checking out sweatshirts. The salesman finally asks if he can help us. And Willie hands him three more sneakers he'd like to try on. I ask for them in my size, too. It's nice being able to afford things.

Maybe it's the fat woman who walks into the store and everyone staring at her like she shouldn't have. Or maybe it's the sneakers. Willie kept saying he looked better in his. I know what Pops would have said to me: "Those sneakers were made for your feet."

"I'll be back," I tell Willie.

He knows why I have to go. But he says he wouldn't if he was me. "Your pops is probably eating something somewhere."

Our friends laugh when he says that.

I leave the store, walking at first. Running when I don't see my dad. He's not where I left him. Not sitting at the table with the umbrella over it, or on the green bench in front of the jeans store, either. I look up the street. Down the block. I even go in the opposite direction. Then I'm back where I left him, standing on the curb—thinking the worst.

We don't have cells. We can't afford them. And I'm with him all the time, unless I'm at school. "Dad! Dad!" I'm screaming.

People want to know if I'm okay.

"No," I say, when the fourth person asks.

"Was your dad wearing a red shirt with a white collar?" a man asks.

I just look at him.

"Was he a big guy—fat?" His arms go out in both directions like my dad is the size of a tank.

"Yeah."

He points up the street. "I saw him, sitting by the curb. The heat got to him, I think. So some people helped him to his feet; got him over to a table back there."

I take off. Yelling for him the whole way. Finally, at this restaurant where the sign out front has a picture of a fish with a pipe between his lips, I see Pops, sitting, fanning himself. Six glasses of ice water are on the table. People are asking if he's okay. Willie would call me a baby, but I hug him so hard he has to ask me to let him breathe.

He's okay, a few people say. "Almost passed out, but we held on to him."

They're standing around Pops like they know him. "He said you were up the street. We were just coming for you."

A woman in a black halter and a guy in a suit ask Pops if he wants to go to the hospital. "We'll call an ambulance, or take you ourselves."

"We have to get sneakers."

"No we don't," I say.

He drinks more ice water. "Yeah, we do. I promised."

I don't want them now. "Willie's getting the same ones, the exact same color."

"You gonna look better in yours," he says, trying to stand.

One man's name is Neil. He bends down. He's got a solution. "Let me drive you two up there. I'll stick around. Drive you home, too."

I look at him. Pops does too. "My car . . ."

His wife asks for our car keys. "I'll follow my husband and we'll get that home too. Just tell me where it is."

"I swear. I am so embarrassed." He digs in his pocket for the keys. The ad falls out. "Gonna lose this weight. I swear. I promise."

The guy stands. So does his wife. They start to help Pops get up; I do too. Then three other guys walk over. "Need some help?"

I always help my dad. But I can't do it by myself, not today. "Sure," I say, watching them help Pops to the car.

He is wider than our washing machine and dryer put side by side. But his smile is even bigger than that when the people walking with us ask him about me. Everything hurts on him, I can tell. But he keeps his head up. And he winks at me when he tells them I made high honor roll last semester. "For the fifth year in a row."

I think about Willie. I think about all my friends and what they will say when we get home and they see strangers helping Pops into the house. But Pops is thinking about my sneakers. "They still got the red ones, right?"

"Right." I squeeze into the back of the car—a silver Mercedes 360 with a sunroof. I lean close to his head, listening to him breathe, once he gets in. "They're the best sneakers in the store," I tell him.

"For the best boy in the world," he says.

Willie would say I'm a wuss, a punk, or something worse, but I move even closer and kiss my dad on the side of his neck. I am not embarrassed. This is my father. I'm his son. And we're doing alright, thank you very much.

STUCK WITH ME

Pimples
Mom telling me I stink
Girls saying I ain't—
Tall enough
Fly enough
That I can't jump and shoot the ball high enough
That's me
Stuck in puberty
Shaving hairs I ain't even got
Waving at girls that say I better not tell nobody that
    they know me
Living in the shower
Hiding magazines
Staying up half the night looking at websites not
    meant for me
Texting girls who never text me back

Knowing I would never treat them like that
Glasses on my nose
Braces on my teeth
Everyone complaining how I eat and eat and eat
But who cares how unfair life can be?
Stuck in puberty
All alone
Just me
    and me.

THE SAME OLD THING

My father leaves the office every day at ten p.m.
My mother complains,
But tomorrow he'll do the same thing again.
Walk in late,
Kiss her on the face,
Ask about my day,
Pray over microwave chicken, asparagus sticks, and
    mashed potatoes from a bag.
Dag.
You'd think he could do better than that.

DON'T READ THIS

Nov. 15

SOME GUYS KEEP DIARIES. My brother TJ says only punks do. Well, I don't have to keep hiding my diaries from people now. I'm done with 'em; for good. Done with everything, even waking up every day pretending like living is fun.

Nov. 18

I was gonna give Derrick my iPod, but he says it's too old. He's seven; everything is older than he is. Little brothers are a pain.

Nov. 20

I think I'm gonna to do it; on Christmas Day. Reynolds says absolutely not. I'll ruin everyone's Christmas forever.

I know. But that's my favorite holiday. I won't be afraid if I do it then. The turkey will be in the oven, stuffed. The ham will be done and so will the pies. I usually hate it when Aunt Betty cooks chitlins. They stink. But I won't mind this year. I want it to be that way, all the smells that I'm used to, hanging around the house when it happens.

Nov. 21

Mom wants me to take an SAT prep course. Why?

Nov. 22

I don't know what I'm gonna do with Justin's things. They're still in his closet. Reynolds won't take clothes— not mine, not Justin's for sure. He says it's morbid. But he took some CDs, the tennis racket I got last summer, and some games. Here's what I'm wondering. If I had gone first, would Justin be trying to follow me? I think he would. A half a twin is never a whole person.

Nov. 23

Here's what I figured. It's gotta be quick. It can't involve blood. And pills are out of the question.

Nov. 24

Reynolds wants to know why I don't blog. Diaries are

for you. Blogs are for everyone else. Justin would understand. He was sorta different, too, carrying that dictionary on him all the time. Everything had to be perfect, even his spelling. Now here I am trying to be like him and hating it. That spelling club I joined makes things even worse. Now for sure people at school will say I am weird.

Nov. 25

Thanksgiving.

I was having fun, and then Mr. E showed up. It wasn't fair, *him* being there, ruining everything. Before we ate we had to say what we remembered and loved about Justin. I skipped my turn. Dad asked if I was okay. I told him I was *perfect*. That was Justin's favorite word. His biggest lie, too. If he was perfect he'd still be here, alive, telling everybody at the table what happened to him.

Nov. 27

I have to slow down on my giving. Mom was in my room, and she wanted to know where my things were. I said the first thing that came to my mind: that Reynolds's dad got laid off. She kissed me for being a good friend. Then she went to Justin's closet. It's still full. *Do you think Reynolds wants some of these, too?* she asked me.

They haven't gotten rid of any of his things. They try,

but it's for me to do, I tell them. I'm the only one who knows who should get what. But every time I start to do it, I have to stop. His smells are still in his clothes, so how can I throw 'em away? Mom and Dad don't fight me on it, because they don't want to go through his things anyhow. Besides, they have me—an exact copy—not the real thing, but just as good—to keep them from being so sad.

Nov. 29

Somebody is telling my business. A girl at school walked up to me, asking if it was true that I was going to kill myself. I told her that just because Justin and I are twins doesn't mean we do everything alike. She said she was glad because it would be awful if I did it too. Awful is being all by yourself, without your shadow. Awful is being in the spelling club when you know you aren't a good speller, and being sad all the time too.

Sometimes I hate him for what he did.

Nov. 30

Saw Mr. E. Crossed the street as fast as I could. He had a lot of nerve trying to speak to me.

Dec. 1

I bought a rope today.

Dec. 2

TJ came into our room. He just stood there watching TV with me for a while. He was trying to be nice, I think. He told me I could go shoot pool with him and his friends. But I've made up my mind. I will clear out Justin's closet today.

Dec. 2, 1:30 a.m.

All of his pockets are empty. No change. No candy, lint—nothing. That's how Justin is. Was. Perfect. Liar. Everything always looked just right. But it wasn't. He could have told me, though. No secrets, we always said. Then he swallows Mom's pills; downs a pint on top of that. I could kill him, if he wasn't dead. Lots of people had it worse than him. Like me. It's worse for me. Now I don't have anybody to talk to about it.

Dec. 2, 2:38 a.m.

Found something today. *The Astronomers Club Handbook*. TJ saw me reading it on the john. Dad made us join that dumb club. Mr. E said it would be good for us. He lied.

Dec. 3

Reynolds says if he were me, he'd poison himself. *Ropes hurt*. He was lying across Justin's bed when he said it. He's the only one besides family that I'd let do that. We three hung out together. "The weird club," TJ called us. We had telescopes and stars, our laptops and Madden games. And when it got too tough at school, we had each other.

I feel bad for Reynolds. He doesn't know why I'm doing this. When I'm gone, he'll be mad, just like I was when I found out why Justin killed himself. Reynolds isn't in the astronomy club. Never has been. His father didn't like the looks of Mr. E. I keep trying to tell Reynolds. I try to tell my parents too about what Mr. E. did. But I can't. It's my fault. I had a feeling that something wasn't right. Mr. E liked his curls too much.

Dec. 4, 3 p.m.

TJ caught me burning my old diaries. He gave me this funny look. *Why?*

I ran out of things to say.

He told Dad that something was up with me. Dad spent two hours in my room, talking, mostly about Justin. He still can't figure out why Justin did it.

I see why Justin didn't tell on Mr. E. It's hard to say out loud that you were . . . that somebody made you . . . I can't even write the words. Hate to think about it. What's it matter now, anyhow? He killed us both.

Dec. 4, 6 p.m.

I wish they would quit coming in here, sitting in my room, watching me. *What's bugging you? If you do something crazy, it will kill us,* they say. *I am not crazy. I am perfect.* That did it for them. They are calling the doctor tomorrow and making an appointment for me. But I already have an appointment.

Dec. 4, 10 p.m.

They're baaaack. They came up with a date for clearing out the rest of Justin's things. January 1. *A new year. A new start.* Dad came up with that one. Mom opened Justin's closet and said it looked like he was spending the night at a friend's and would be coming home any minute. She picked up his spelling bee medals. She thanked me for keeping his side of the room so neat and dusted. I have to. In his letter he asked me to keep everything in place. I'm not like him. My side of the room used to always stay messy. It's hard, keeping it this way—perfect. I try to do what he wanted, except for one thing. I never did give Jennifer her letter. Mom and Dad got theirs. I got mine, so did Reynolds. But not her. *Don't Read This, James* he wrote on the outside of her envelope. He should have known better. Jennifer was not his best friend. Jennifer was not his twin. She wasn't even a girl that would date someone like him, so why did he tell her what Mr. E did to him? If he had told me earlier, he'd be alive. And Mr. E . . . we woulda figured out what to do with him. Sometimes I wonder if the other kids in the club know how much he likes the planetarium.

Dec. 4, 11:59 p.m.

The note. I woke up thinking about it. Can't forget what it said. I think he wrote it to her 'cause I didn't listen when he tried to tell me all those times. *You never listen.* He always said that to me. *I don't want to hear about Mr. E, Justin,* I said the night before he committed suicide. Complaining about Mr. E and his boring astronomy club was our thing. Skipping astronomy club meetings twice a month was my thing. Justin, you always covered for me. Made up a good reason why I wasn't there. Mr. E never told or complained. Now I know why.

Dec. 6

No school today. Too much snow. I rode my sled. I used the snowblower on our neighbors' pavement, then went with Reynolds to shovel sidewalks when I ran out of gas. We made ninety bucks each. I bought Derrick a new video game. It was a good day.

Dec. 7

More snow. I wish it would quit. Too much snow means I spend more time in my room. I dusted and waxed. Then I got mad at Justin because that is him, not me. The other day I was in the kitchen putting food away for Mom. I put the soup away just like he did—alphabetical order, six rows behind the baked beans, Capri Sun, and the crackers. TJ is right. Justin was weird. I am weird. Now I'm weird all by myself.

Dec. 7, 6:30 p.m.

He texted me. I deleted it. Then I went to the bathroom and puked.

Dec. 8

My cooking teacher asked me to stay after class today. She says there is this crazy rumor about me planning to do something stupid. People don't like to say suicide. Reynolds says *When you do it,* or *When you bite the bullet.* I took out my cell and showed Mrs. Miller a picture of my Wii game, the one I already gave away. *I just got this. And nobody's gonna end up with it but me.* She is the best. She took some cold spaghetti out of the fridge, and she and I ate it. I hate lying to her. She is the person I go to a lot here. She's not like other grown-ups—your secrets are safe with her.

Dec. 9

There's a website with a clock on it, for people like me. You set the day. You set the month. You kill yourself right on time. That's ghoulish. It should be against the law, too. When I write my note and tell people why I did what I did, I'll bring up that clock. When you are planning to kill yourself, you have a clock ticking in your head already. It doesn't bother you, that clock. It excites you; calms you sort of, knowing that it will all be over soon. But a clock on the Web counting dead bodies around the world—that's just plain wrong.

Dec. 10

Sheryl Mitchell called me. She never called me in her whole entire life. No girl has. She wanted to know if it was true. I made her come right out and ask, not hint around like she was doing. She never knew anyone who had done it before, so she asked how I was going to do it. I lied and said I hadn't made up my mind. *When I know, would I tell her?* she asked. *Not that I think you should do it. But if you are going to do it, I want to put it on my blog. I like to be first on things.* I had to think about that one. Then I said sure. I would call her right before I did it. Then she could e-mail everyone else. That's a good plan, I think. It saves me the trouble of setting my computer to send e-mail afterward.

Dec. 11

If you want girls to blow up your cell, just tell one of them that you're going to kill yourself. That's what I was thinking today when Sarinda called me. I've never given her my number. I didn't ask how she got it. She just said she had *heard*. And she was calling to cheer me up. She was the second girl to call in two days. I'm thinking that more girls will text or call. I was never popular. I'm starting to be, I guess.

Dec. 11, noon

I'm supposed to see a therapist next week. Mr. E needs a therapist, not me.

Dec. 11, 2:30 pm.

I won't do what Justin did. I will leave my diary for my folks. They will read it and find out about Mr. E. And do what? Something horrible . . . I want something bad to happen to him.

Dec. 11, 4 p.m.

I think I want to have a party. Reynolds says I need to say good-bye to people before I go. He's right. Justin didn't do that. He just mopped the kitchen, cleaned our room, and left.

Bad news, say my parents. Good news to me. Therapist is on hold. Insurance problems.

Dec. 12

No mistakes. Everything must be one hundred percent perfect.

Dec. 12, 11:50 a.m.

I was in the bathtub when I remembered. The first time Justin met Mr. E he was afraid of him. Dad left us with him at the club. I caught him rubbing Justin's curls. Three years in that club. Three years of him hurting Justin, or was it two years, or six months? My brain won't shut up. I still have a million questions for you, bro. So I have to go and be with you; to say in person that I'm sorry; to ask you when it started and was it my fault . . . I hated astronomy club. Stars aren't as much fun as racing cars or playing video games. That's what I thought.

Dec. 13

I bought another rope today. Three, in fact. Reynolds says nylon is for Double Dutch. I trashed that one. Two is plenty.

Dec. 14

TJ came in my room and saw me shaking like a leaf, so he took me downtown to get my mind off things. Surprise. He bought me a new diary. He must really be scared for me.

Dec. 15

The girl with the blog stopped me in the hall today. She wanted to know if I had any particular date in mind. Of course. But I didn't tell her. There is something creepy about her. Next she'll probably ask me to take a picture of myself doing it.

Dec. 16

You can find anything on the Internet, even how to make the perfect knot. For a while today I was on suicide prevention sites—there's a lot of those. If I had read them before, would I still be planning this? Would Justin be alive if Mr. E had picked me instead? There was good information on the sites. But the clock is ticking, and Justin is waiting.

Another text.

Hi.
Mr. E.

I'm wondering if I should tell his wife. I see them together at the mall sometimes. *A good family man*, Dad calls him. I wonder who will be next?

Dec. 17

Christmas will be the day. Any day I do it will be a bad day for my folks, so I might as well pick a day that is good for me. I'll do it after the presents. After Aunt Betty comes by and smells up the place. After they drink their cocktails, maybe around two o'clock. No, I'll do it later. After their food settles.

Dec. 19

Yesterday I was so happy I played with Derrick all day long. It'll be a relief, being a twin again.

Dec. 20

The principal called. Mrs. Miller went to him about me. She told him I wasn't my old self; that I looked sad and was much too quiet lately. That got the other teachers talking. They notice I don't do my homework. They are hearing things from other kids. *Have my grades dropped? I asked my parents. Have I missed school or quit any clubs? No! I'm fine! So get out of my room!*

Dad said Mr. E wants to know when I'm coming back

to astronomy club. I got sick. Mom cleaned up the mess. *I'm getting the flu*, I said, covering my nose from the stink. Then I remembered. Justin threw up the last time he went to astronomy club. *I'm getting the flu*, that's what he said. *It's nothing*. The next day he was gone.

Dec. 21

Reynolds has been avoiding me. He says he's preparing himself. But he did IM me a picture of a license plate. It said: Weird 1. I asked him to make a Weird 2 and 3. He was already working on it.

Dec. 21, 4 p.m.

That girl who wants to blog about me texted. I didn't answer. I have decided to keep my plans to myself. Just Justin and my diary will know what I'm up to. And Reynolds, of course.

Dec. 22

I gave TJ Justin's medals and his jewelry. TJ thought I would always keep them. He asked if I wanted to go jogging. I don't jog. He never asks, either. *What's up with you?* he said. Then he went running. When he came back he showered and then came in my room. I tried to get him to leave, but he wouldn't. He stayed in Justin's bed all night.

Dec. 23, 11 a.m.

I should tell TJ. But he would say what I say to myself sometimes. *Why did you keep quiet for so long? How come you didn't notice? He was your responsibility, the youngest twin. No way would he let that happen to you.*

Dec. 23

The last day of school. Yes!

Dec. 24

Dry run. Rope. Chair. Water to drink. (Don't know why.)

I put everything away afterward. Even cleaned the toilet after I got sick. Perfect.

Dec. 25

Reynolds says for me not to do it. I asked if he'd ever tell. My secrets are always safe with him, he says. But he thinks maybe this is a bad idea.

Dec. 25, 10 a.m.

I can't.

Dec. 25, 11 a.m.

I wrote three notes. One to my parents. One to

Reynolds. One to TJ and Derrick. I started one to Mr. E. I need more time to write that one.

Dec. 25, 1 p.m.

I texted the girl who needs to know when I'll be done and over with. She wasn't happy or sad about it. But she wanted too many details. *Come watch. It happens at 7:00*, I wrote, lying. But I swear she would have come if I had given her our address.

Dec. 25, 2 p.m.

My parents say for me to quit pacing around and go do something. I *am* doing something. I'm waiting.

Dec. 25, 4 p.m.

Dinner was great! Dessert was too: cheesecake and chocolate raspberry pie just for me. I love surprises!

Dec. 25, 4:30 p.m.

I texted her. She never answered. I'll send her Mr. E's letter and she can post it. Now I know why Justin wanted Jennifer to have the note. You just want somebody, anybody, to know the truth.

Dec. 25, 4:45 p.m.

If I don't do it, will I ever feel better?

Dec 25, 10 p.m.

TJ won't leave my room. He's been in and out of here since lunchtime. I'll have to come up with a new date.

Dec. 25, 11 p.m.

Blog girl is not happy. She wants a rain date.

Dec. 27

I feel really good. Great. TJ and I went jogging in the snow. I made pancakes with Derrick. Then I went to the mall with Dad. I'm so glad I'm not dead!!!!

Dec. 28

Reynolds stayed all day. He is surprised at how happy I am. Killing myself was a stupid idea. No shower since I made the decision. Dirty clothes on the floor. The old me is back!

Dec. 29

All I want to do is go and go and go. Derrick and I made snow angels. Reynolds and I hit the mall, then went for pizza and ended up snowboarding with some kids from school. I haven't even thought much about Justin today. And I asked my parents for paint to redo our room. Even

Mr. E doesn't bother me anymore. He texted me twice and I gave him a piece of my mind.

Dec. 30

Hung out with friends today. Couldn't shut up. Couldn't sit down. Had a blast. Tomorrow we go to the science museum. After that, bowling. Fun. I want to have fun, fun, fun, fun.

Dec. 31, 6 a.m.

Bad day.

Dec. 31, 3 p.m.

Still in bed.

Dec. 31, 11:30 p.m.

Justin on my mind. Another year without him. Black-eyed peas, rice, and greens cooking on the stove. No appetite. A twin who's really not a twin. Saw Mr. E yesterday. He winked when he passed me on the street. His wife never noticed. I deleted the letter I was writing to him. What's the use?

Jan. 1

It is the worst—dying by rope. Being squeezed to

death. Feeling the burn. Kicking and twisting; trying to come down; knowing you can't get down. Spinning. The rope getting tighter, making you wish you were dead while you are praying to God you won't die.

TJ thinks diaries are stupid. He used to, until he found mine. And he found me. And they found out about Mr. E.

March 12

Twins are twins forever. Justin is dead, but not me. Weird 2 and Weird 3 will always be together. That's what I tell people now. But I am happy not to be dead. Glad that our secret is out. No more pills. No more ropes. No way for Mr. E to hurt boys anymore.

March 13

The therapist says it's okay to talk about Justin and Mr. E. To cry and be mad too. I didn't do anything wrong, he says. And neither did Justin. I'm trying to believe that. It's hard, some days.

TJ says he would never keep a diary. But he bought this one for me anyhow. I am lucky, I told him this morning. I have two brothers, and a best friend—Reynolds—whose big mouth comes in handy sometimes.

MESSAGES

I.

What I like about you

Your lips
Your eyes
Your thighs
Wow

II.

You should have known

To the guys on my block who told me not to tell,
Oops.

III.

Too many girls

To the girls who text me,
Then get mad when I don't text back,
Oh well.

IV.
My ride

I love my car
I like you
Don't be hatin' 'cause my car's my boo.

V.
The first time

The first time I kissed you
Was the first time I kissed
I'll do better next time.

I'M NOT SUPPOSED TO

I'm not supposed to love you but I do
Who
Makes up these rules anyhow
Cows?
Chickens?
People afraid of the dark?
Old farts?
Maybe one day they will say it's okay
That love doesn't always have to dress up in gray
That you and I can say what they always say
I love you
Today
And always.

GIRLS MAKE YOU WEAK

IT WAS PASSED DOWN TO ME. Just like my uncles' blue eyes, my grandfather's flat feet, and my dad's big nose. All the men in our family have it. And it didn't skip one generation, either. The men call it the cheating gene. They say it's built into our DNA. The women in our family say we're just nasty, sniffing after every skirt in town. But we were born this way. I swear. Even my three-year-old cousin Richie has it. A woman walks into the room and he goes after her. The next thing we know he's sitting on her lap, rubbing the side of her face, getting all the kisses he wants. Sometimes he even goes for her thighs. "He just likes how stockings feel," his mom will say. We guys tell her that he's gonna be a leg man—just like the rest of us.

I started off like Richie; that's what Mom says. Only I was younger—two years old and cute enough to model.

Now I'm seventeen. In the eleventh grade. And getting all the girls—even the ones that belong to my boys.

"Hey, Tyler. I texted you last night. Why didn't you text me back?"

It takes me a minute to think up an answer. "Aw, man . . . I meant to. Sorry." If you tell a girl the truth, she says it's a lie anyhow. So I tell them what they want to hear. It just makes life easier. "I'll hit you up later."

Monique's arms go around my waist, and her belly pushes into me. My phone vibrates, over and over again. It's in my front pocket. She feels it. And just gets closer. "You know too many girls," she says, digging in my pants, grabbing at my phone.

Girls play around too much. Especially ones like Monique. "Hey. Don't do that." I push her hands away. But she has nails, long ones with diamonds on the tips. "Don't scratch me, girl."

"Just let me see it."

"Huh?"

"Come on." She's on me again. I don't like her, but I like how it feels with her so close that if she sweats I'll feel it. "Monique . . ."

"It's just a phone, right?" Her fingers dig around in my pocket. "Everyone's got one." Her other hand goes around my back. "So what do you care if I see who's on the other end? I know everybody at this school anyhow."

I'm taller than she is, six-one to be exact. She's like five-five, and pretty, I guess you could say. But anybody can have pretty, you know what I mean? There's tons of those here. I walk by 'em every day. They give me their numbers and I pass them on to my boys. Beautiful, that's what I'm after. The top of the line—Bentleys, Range Rovers, that's my type. "Hey, Monique, quit that," I say, shoving her.

Attitude. I knew it was coming. It's not just a black-girl thing, either. White girls have it now, too. That's why sometimes I just go for the foreigners. You know, the girls that snuck across the border a few years back. Or the ones whose parents wait on you at the hospital, but you need the nurse to tell you what they're saying.

"You're not all that cute." Monique looks me up and down and gives me the finger. "And you probably have some disease anyhow." She stares at my phone, then lowers her eyes. "You know what they call girls that do what you do?"

I'm waiting for her to say it. She doesn't, because if she does, we're done.

"Just text me sometimes, okay?"

"I will. Seriously."

She takes a pen out of her backpack, lifts my hand, and writes her number on my palm in red ink. "Just in case you forgot," she says. And then she's gone. But men in our family are like airports: as soon as one plane takes off, here comes another.

"Tyler. Hi."

Beautiful. Celeste Johnson Nichols is beautiful. She would never rub up on a guy, but man, you wish she would. "Hey, Celeste." I pull out my phone and keep moving. You can't just stop for a girl like her. She expects it, you know. You can't give her the upper hand either—that's what my uncles say.

"Wait up."

She's following me. But not the way Monique does, all desperate-like. She takes her time. So I step it up. If she wants to talk to me, she's gonna have to hustle.

Celeste and I went together all last year. We both decided to call it quits and just be friends. She did not like the way girls blew up my cell. I did not like the way I acted around her, like I could not live without her. We said we would just be friends. But she plays too many games. Like she has a cell, but she blocks my number. She lives six blocks from my house, but if I come by, her mom always says she's not home. In the hallway, Celeste might speak to me; she might not. Then one day out the blue, she will do what she just did—ask me to hold up. I hate that. Because when she does, I get to thinking . . . maybe.

"Tyler. This is silly. Just stop."

I don't want to, but I do. "Hey, what's up?" But then I'm staring into her eyes. I can't help it. Her eyes are almost as pretty as mine. Mix her chocolate brown with my blue eyes, and wow. She said that to me once. She said when we get married and have babies they are going to be the prettiest kids ever. Why would a girl talk like that? What guy do you know wants to get married or talk about babies at my age? Besides, she'll say something nice then ignore me in class or tell the lab teacher she wants another partner. Why would she do that? Because she can, my father said once. "So set her straight," he told me. "Let her know who's in charge."

When you are as tall as I am, you like looking down at the world. It makes you feel better, stronger, smarter than everyone else. Only Celeste is my kryptonite. Walking with her makes me feel like a Hummer with a grenade underneath. Any second it's like she is going to say something, do something that will make me feel two inches tall. I hate that.

Celeste plays with her gold necklace and stands too close to me. "So what are you doing this summer?"

I try to play it cool. "I don't know. My dad wants to go to the shore, Mom wants Vegas."

She stares at my feet. "I like your shoes. Are they new?"

She knows what she's doing. I've got this thing for shoes, not sneakers. Everyone's got those. Me, I have like sixty-five pair of shoes. People wait for me to come to school just to see what I have on my feet. So if you say something about them, it's like I get high. "Thanks." I stare at my blue shoes. "My brother sent them from Cali— Rodeo Drive, I think."

Guys passing by say hello to me. But I see their eyes stopping on her best parts. One dude just shakes his head. That's all you can do when you see a girl like her, because you know the guy that gets her is lucky. And you're just hoping he screws up, so you can get a chance.

"What you doing this weekend?" I did not mean to ask her that.

"I don't know. Nothing, I guess."

See? This is how she plays the game. She says she's not doing anything, then all of a sudden she's busy when I ask her out. Well, I'm busy too. "Miya and I are going to do something. I'm not sure what."

"Oh."

I like it when I get to her first. She does it to me all the time.

"She's . . . cute," she says, but I can tell that she doesn't believe that. Celeste waves to a guy who's driving out of the school parking lot in a Benz. "Hold on," she tells me, and then takes her time walking over to him.

Celeste used to run track, so the muscles in her legs flex when she walks. And she used to dance ballet and tap, so her back is straight and her neck is long. It's more like she is floating than walking, showing off more than just trying to get someplace.

She makes me wait ten minutes before she stops laughing and talking to him. So am I supposed to stand here doing nothing? "Hey, Angelina, wait up," I say, watching Celeste watch me while she's still talking to him.

"What's up, blue eyes?"

You cannot just let a girl like Angelina pass you by. So I pull her away from her friends and give her the once-over. I let her know how good she looks. How lucky her boyfriend is. She speaks soft. To hear her, you've got to get close to her. So I get close; then a little bit closer. "What you up to, girl? You got the same number?"

Angelina's hair is down to her waist. And it's real. But that's not what I'm looking at. I'm staring at that dress fitting her like the numbers on a cell—any smaller and she'd be in trouble. She plays with her hair while she's talking. "Same number. Only guys with pretty eyes can call me, though." I take a few strands and start playing too. When I look over at Celeste, she's heading for the gate, leaving the school grounds. I start running. "Talk to you later, Angelina."

I hate this crap. I can get any girl I want. "Wait up, Celeste."

She keeps walking. It's one of those I'm-mad-at-you walks, with her feet practically stomping the ground, but with her talking to me like everything is fine. We walk a block or two without saying anything. But I'm thinking: I can do better, way better than her. Then she stops and asks if there's something in her eye. I lean over her, blowing at the hair in the corner of her eye. When I'm done, it's her lips I'm staring at. Celeste has these big pretty lips that always shine from gloss and the sun reflecting off them. She licks them. I clear my throat. She's explaining that if a girl plays her cards right, she can get a dude to do whatever she wants. I'm trying to make her understand that there are just too many girls around who will do what a guy says. "So he'd have to be nuts to stick with a girl who wants to play hard, when he can be with a ton of girls who just like to play."

"Thanks," she says.

"You okay?"

Her eyes are watering. "You sure there's nothing in my eye? Man, it hurts."

I pull down her bottom eyelid, like my mother does for me. I pick at her lashes, to see which ones might still be loose. She's doing this on purpose, I swear. But I like it, even though I hate it. I am wondering when she is going to hit the beach with me; let me oil her skin. It's the color of honey in the winter; apple butter brown in the summer.

"Tyler!"

Some girls' voices are like acid; they eat right through you.

I turn around. "What?"

Celeste pushes my hand away. "Don't talk to her like that."

"I waited for you last night."

"I . . . I . . ." Girls love drama. "I wasn't home. Text me."

The car Sabrina's riding in takes off, with Sabrina's finger still hanging out the car window, pointing toward the clouds.

"So how many girlfriends *do* you have?" Celeste asks.

"I don't do girlfriends."

"Monique—is she your girl?"

"I told you. No girlfriends. Just friends."

"What about Asia? Miya?"

"Friends. I'm done having girlfriends."

When she changes the subject she walks a little closer to me. "So *what* are you doing this weekend? I forget."

It's a trick question, I know it. Only I'm not sure how to answer, especially since I already did. "Who knows?"

She says it's a pity that I'm busy with Miya this

weekend, because if I weren't, she and I could hang out, see a movie or something.

Before I say it, I tell myself not to say it. But I am stupid for her. My dad says it all the time. "The dumbest man in the family," he and my uncles call me. But I am just like them. I love girls—loads of them. It's just that I've got this thing for Celeste. "What about next Saturday?" I say.

She smiles. "I don't know."

"What?"

"I was just asking. I'm not a hundred percent sure of my plans."

You are stupid man, just stupid, I tell myself.

It's a game. But I know how to play too. We've been playing it since last year, when I figured out that you cannot give too much of yourself to a girl. Some girls are like that, my uncles say. They know they got you, so they mess with your head. "They'll ruin your mojo if you let them, boy."

"Listen," I say, kissing the side of her lips. "Unblock my number."

Her mouth opens just a little, and I get the sweetest kiss. I try to make it last. "Why should I?" she says, breathing hard, putting her arms around me, making me wish we were back together again.

She smells like coconuts. And I like coconuts, so I put

my nose to her neck and sniff and kiss. "Because you know you want to," I say, surprised when she finds my lips and kisses me again.

"Do I?"

"Yeah," I say, hardly getting the word out.

"Or do you just want me to do it?"

We both are silent. Then she's like, "If you ask me again, I will." She smiles. "Unblock your number, I mean."

If I say yes, she will just say no. So I don't ask her to. I can't. Girls will make you soft. They will give you the run-around. Screw with your head. Celeste does this to me all the time. I step back from her. "I need to go," I say, even though I don't want to.

She looks hurt. Then she walks onto her porch, digs around in her purse for her keys, and says, "I was going to unblock it, if only you had asked."

"If she wants to be with you, let her do the work," I hear my brother saying.

My friend Terence's voice is in my head, too. "Quit letting that girl play you."

"Don't be no fool," my uncles always say.

Celeste is the only girl I've ever loved. The only one whose picture is in my bedroom and my wallet, too. I'm just about ready to tell her to unblock me, to make a fool outta me even, when all of a sudden who comes walking up the street but Angelina. It's like God sent her to stop me before I did something crazy.

Angelina struts. Her heels scrape the ground and her feet stomp, so you always know when she's coming. She and Celeste both have on yellow today. One yellow tells you to hold up, slow down. The other is like the sun, hot and getting hotter.

Celeste and I both stare at her. But I am the one who follows her. "Angelina, hold up."

My lips are on her lips before she says a word.

"Man. They're soft as butter," she says.

It would have been better if Celeste had heard her.

I put my arm over Angelina's shoulder. We start walking, and her hips move like music is playing somewhere. A horn beeps. She waves. Celeste stares over at the two of us.

At the corner, while we wait for the light to change, she whispers in my ear, saying something in Spanish.

Celeste can't keep her eyes off of us.

Angelina squeezes me tighter. Then she stops and stares into my eyes. "You are so fine. And your eyes. Oh my goodness. They are so pretty."

I could kiss Angelina again. I can tell she wants me to. And it would teach Celeste a lesson, that she's not the only girl around.

I start walking, asking Angelina what she's doing later

on. I'm not listening to her, though. I'm thinking about Celeste, wondering if she really would have unblocked her phone. No, I think, asking Angelina if she wants to go get something to eat, ignoring the part of me that wants to turn around and go back and be with Celeste. I'm a good dude, Celeste needs to know that. I can get any girl I want. She needs to know that too. The men in our family got it like that. Blue eyes, brown-skinned, and fine gives you options. Gets you any girl, any place, any time, I think, looking back at Celeste opening her front door. Wondering why some girls like to play games. Hoping Angelina don't think I'm paying for her food.

LOOK

Go ahead
Look
I would too
If I saw what you see
Me
Sixteen
Sexy as can be
Me
So fine I'm just about pretty
Go ahead
Look
I work hard to get this way
Running cross-country
Playing baseball, football
Lifting weights every day
Go ahead

Look
If you lucky I'll walk your way
Maybe ask you for your number
Maybe kiss those lips today
Go ahead
Look
It's okay

CHOCOLATE CINNAMON BEIGE

Chocolate
Cinnamon
Beige
A girl like you make me wanna behave better than I
    ever have before.
Boy, what you gonna have me doing next?
Studying for tests with you?
Holding your hand; taking you to the zoo?
Alright,
Okay,
I'm down with that.
Anything for you,
My
Chocolate
Cinnamon
Beige-colored boo.

Alright,
Okay,
You done gone and made me say it now, too.
I love you,
My Chocolate
Cinnamon
Beige-colored boo

INFECTED

Dear Uncle Arin:

    I SCREWED UP! Bad. And there's nothing you or nobody else can do to fix it.

    I'm in my counselor's office—the one at school who you always said you liked. I got some news last week that she said I should tell you. That's why I'm writing this letter. If you read e-mail, I woulda e-mailed you. If you texted like Aunt April, I woulda texted you. But I couldn't just call you up on the phone and tell you nothing like this. No way.

    First let me say that I'm glad you let me come to live with you. New York is way better than Erie. And being in a school for kids like me, who play music and who dance or act or paint, is the best thing that ever happened to me. So thanks.

Uncle Arin, I know you told me to slow down. I know you said I ain't have to eat the whole apple at once—but I'm from a small town. We don't have hardly none of the things they have in New York. Even the people are different here. They walk fast. . . . They talk fast. Time even seems to go faster here. So I guess it only makes sense that I got fast, too. When I told my friends back home that I had five girlfriends in three months, they swore I was lying. I was, a little, and you was right when you told me that New York was gonna give me plenty of real stories to tell, so I could quit sending lies home. I see what you mean, now. I got a story none of my friends is gonna believe. I wish it was a lie. I wish it was a dream. But it ain't.

Remember how I was before I came here? I was a really good student—all B's and A's. I stayed in the house all the time 'cause Mom said I wasn't like the other kids around our way. And I wasn't. I liked to write poetry, not rap. I loved to read, too.

Like I said, you did me a favor, bringing me to New York. But you messed my life up too. I didn't drink when I was back in Erie. And I never smoked. I hated the way cigarettes smelled. But here I tasted everything I could, even sushi. Even menthol cigarettes. My friends changed, too. I was used to kids in black and white. Then

I came here and met kids from everywhere: Vietnam, North Korea, Japan. Nigeria, Ethiopia, and Greece. You reminded me that the Islands live here—so it was nothing for me to hang with kids from Barbados and Antigua; to play the steel drums and eat fish with the heads on. They had all kinds of stories. Bet none of theirs can beat mine.

Miss Cox is looking over my shoulder, telling me that I'm stalling. She says she'll dial your number, then put me on the phone, if I like. But I can't do it that way. You might cuss me out. Or cry, even though you say men don't do that.

Okay. So here it is. Remember when I went out a few months ago? You said for me to be home by twelve. You were on the phone that night with Mom, and she heard you and got pissed. You told her that New York time was different than Erie time. That New York City kids were more mature, too. I did not come home until three. I threw up the six beers and the three cranberry vodkas I had drunk. It was our secret, you said, and you promised not to tell Mom or Aunt Carole. And you didn't. You asked where I had been. I lied when I said I was at Jason's house and he and I had been skateboarding on Fifth before we went to a party in the Bronx. You kept asking if I had been with a girl. I lied and said no. My head hurt. I just wanted to shower and go to sleep. Something kept saying, Tell him. Uncle Arin's cool. He'll understand. But I was scared. So I just kept things to myself.

You know, I think you had a premonition, 'cause the next day you asked me again, remember? "Was you with a girl? Did you do like I said?" I said no, but the rest of that day I stayed away from you. I figured you'd be able to tell after a while that I had been lying, kind of. I mean, I was with a girl. But I ain't do what you said I should—protect myself. We were just having fun. Drinking. Kissing. You know. And I thought about it for a minute—I mean, they tell you in school to be safe. They tell you on television to stop, think, and take care of your business. Wrap up. But when you are right there at that moment having a good time, you forget stuff. Or you just don't care what happens because you figure it won't happen to you nohow.

Uncle Arin, I'm scared. I wouldn't say that to nobody else in the world but you, 'cause other guys would say I'm weak. I already get called that and worse for writing poetry and playing the violin. But when she called me and told me she was positive and I should get tested too, my heart beat so hard I thought it was gonna bust out my body. It was crazy how she told me. Real calm, you know. She said she was just going to take some pills and get on with her life. Only you take those forever, I know, because they talk about it in school. And if you don't have the money, then what? You ain't rich, us neither. So what do that mean? I don't get any pills to treat my HIV?

They say I'll have the virus forever. That I could maybe even get full-blown AIDS. I went online. I read about it. I saw the pictures. People live longer than before, but . . . I don't want this. I want to hurt her; knock her out. I asked her why was she sleeping around without protecting herself. She asked me why I was.

Miss Cox asked if I knew who gave it to whom. At first I ain't know what she was talking about. "Did you ask the other girls you were with if they had other partners?" It took two hours before I told Miss Cox the truth. That girl wasn't my first. And wrapping up wasn't my style— before, anyhow. Maybe I started it, she said. Or maybe I passed it along. She said that I had a duty to let each girl know that I was infected, otherwise I might as well put a bullet to their heads and shoot, because I was killing them just the same.

Miss Cox says for me to calm down. To talk to my parents and do what the doctors say and maybe everything will be like it was before. But it won't. I got a premonition, too. I think I'll get AIDS. She says I'm just upset, worried about things. But when I was little and my brother got the chicken pox, I got them double bad. When he got a cold,

I got pneumonia—twice. It's always been different for me. My body never could fight off things the way other people's could. But you always said not to worry. That I was smarter, had more talent, that I would be the one to put my parents in a mansion one day. I screwed that up, didn't I?

Please don't call me after you read this. Please don't stop me in the hall or the kitchen and bring it up. I do not want to discuss it. And I ain't ready to tell my parents, so please keep it to yourself. I'm begging you. What's it matter anyhow? What's done is done. If I had to do it again, I'd do different: wrap up, or just forget about doing anything at all, ever.

I know I never say it, but I love you. And I'm sorry. Really, really sorry.

Yours truly,
La'Ron

Dear La'Ron:

First off let me say this: I love you and there's
nothing you and our family can't get through together. HIV
don't have to be no death sentence, but it sure won't be no
picnic for you, either. You were thirteen when you came here
from Erie two years ago. Just a boy. I guess you'll turn into a
man lickety-split now. Sorry 'bout that. Being grown ain't as
much fun as kids think.

I'm writing you back, La'Ron, because I showed your
aunt the letter you left for me. She said I needed to respect
your wishes and give you some space, at least for a day or so.
Y'all both out your minds, that's what I thought at first. Then
I realized I needed a few days for me too. You got HIV on my
watch. So I got some explaining to do myself.

Your aunt asked if I ever had that talk with you. You
know, the one about sex. I asked her if she was nuts. Of
course I did. Remember that day? It was that same week you
came to live with us. She looked at me like I had two heads
when I said that. "You only talked to him once? That's it?"
My father only talked to me once, for five minutes. "Use
these," he said, handing a box of condoms to me. I didn't
even know what they were. I always thought he didn't handle
that thing right. I ain't do any better with you, I see. "Wrap
up, wear a raincoat," those were my exact words. I been
asking myself all day long, was I out my mind giving you

that kind of advice in this day and age? I ain't sixty. I'm only fifty. I shoulda known better. But the truth is, I was never good at talking about things like that, even with my own son. I guess I got lucky with Arthur. Twenty-five and no babies. I shoulda had him talk to you.

I wouldn't tell your aunt, but I liked you having all those girlfriends. A boy who plays the violin and writes poetry got to do something to let the world know he's "all male." And you're so smart, everybody knows that. So I just thought you'd know what to do.

~~AIDS.~~ HIV. How could someone in my family have that? Gay people get that. That's what I always thought. Drug addicts, too. Your aunt's been pulling things off the Internet all day, showing me articles about black people and young people and AIDS. Man, she even showed me how people our age are getting it too. I do not want to talk about this. I want it to go away. And you—one minute I'm crying over you having it, the next minute I'm mad enough to put you on a train and ship you out of town. HIV in my house?! That wasn't never supposed to happen. You shouldn't have nothing like that. You're young. Got your whole life in front of you. Why you? Why us? We're not bad people. We don't do nothing illegal. I try to go to church every once in a while. I don't lie. Don't cheat. Now this happens. What the neighbors gonna say, huh? How's your aunt gonna usher

in church now? We did not deserve this! We were good
to you.

I've written and rewritten this letter three times now.
I want to say the right things. But I can't lie. I'm feeling too
many things to get this letter right. I'm blaming me and
blaming you, and blaming your parents for sending you up
here. And you know what, that girl's parents shoulda kept
a better eye on her, too. A young girl ought to have herself
at home, not out someplace getting laid. You all are all too
young to be having sex anyhow. This mess is proof of that.

La'Ron. What we gonna do, boy? How we gonna fix
this? It's not like that bike I bought you and put together.
There's medicine and doctors. Blood tests and counselors.
Gossip and hurt feelings. And days when you gonna be sick
and tired of all of it. If I said I wasn't scared for you I'd be
lying. But your aunt keeps on saying we can do this. So I
guess we can; we have to, huh?

So now that I've told you off, let me apologize for
letting you down; for sending you out there with nothing
but a few words on how to protect yourself, knowing full
well that ten dictionaries don't got enough words on how
to help a young boy figure out this thing between him, girls,
and his hormones. But what's done is done. Now what?

Let me say this: you done the right thing by telling
us you're HIV positive. Your aunt's right. That's probably

the hardest thing you ever had to do. You coulda hid this from us. You coulda pretended nothing was wrong, and kept having a good time with those girls. But a man takes responsibility for himself, and other people too. I'm hurt, but I'm proud. Now we all got to get busy taking care of you.

Your aunt and I came up with a plan. We gonna ask your parents if you can still live here with us, if that's okay with you. We got the best hospitals in the country right here in New York City. There are all kinds of programs for people with HIV and AIDS. You know your aunt been driving me nuts with all the ways we can get you some help. She even found support groups for kids your age. That's good. But it seems wrong—I mean, fourteen and sixteen-year-olds needing something like that.

La'Ron, I do not want to tell your parents that you have HIV. It's gonna break their hearts. But it's man-up time for both of us, I guess. Thursday your folks are coming here by train. They don't know why, but they know it has to do with you. Some things shouldn't be said over the phone, I think.

Your aunt and I scheduled you an appointment with our doctor and arranged for someone from an AIDS group to sit and meet with all of us. I'm hoping your parents are alright with that. If they're not, I guess they'll be taking you home.

Either way, I got to get up to speed on all this. We all do. Did I tell you there's a hotline? You can call anytime you want to ask questions and talk. Your aunt says she and me can call too; go to a support group even. I don't know. Sitting 'round telling strangers my business ain't me. But who knows. Everything's different now.

La'Ron, I'll be honest, the one thing that keeps me up at night besides you and your situation are those girls you mentioned in your letter. One minute I'm saying they just triflin'. Then I'm thinking they somebody's daughters. I think about them: infected. Teenagers taking medicine for life. Girls that trusted you. That you trusted, maybe. If my baby girl walked into the house and told me she had HIV or AIDS—I swear, I'd wanna kill the dude responsible. Your aunt says it's too early, but I just believe you need to contact them one by one, once you get your head on straight. I know the county's doing that, now that you've passed on their information. But I'm thinking that maybe you need to do it too. It's just a thought. A way to own your part in this; not just walk away from what you did to other people, or what they might have did to you.

You a good boy, La'Ron. You can still do the things in life that you planned. But you right, your life won't never be the same. You will get sick sometimes. Maybe end up in the hospital, too. And you're gonna kick yourself more times than you can count. But we're gonna get through this. Together. Like family. And who knows, maybe you will talk to the kids at school or church after a while. They need to know that what happened to you can happen to them too if they ain't smart.

Well, you did it. You told us. Now it's up to us to take the next step. Like I said when I started this letter, this disease don't have to be no death sentence. There's medicine. There's help. There's us, here for you every step of the way. And there's you, a smart boy who made a big mistake and now is going to make the best life possible.

Soon the sun is gonna be up. I got to finish this letter and go back to bed. I probably won't be able to sleep, though. I still got a lot on my mind. Just like you, I figure.

Love always,
Uncle Arin

SO SHE'S WHITE

Alright
So she's white
That's what I like
A girl who walks by my side
Head up, filled with pride
A girl who looks into my eyes
Like she sees kings rising inside
You crazy if you think I'm dumping her, 'cause I ain't.
See
I'm doing my own thing
Being king over me
Ignoring what you see
A white girl
That you say is all wrong for me
So you best get with this—
What you think won't change a thing,
Until you learn to recognize a king when he's passing by.

MY HOOD

THE POLICE MOST LIKELY wouldn't agree, but the hotter it gets in North Philadelphia, the better. Philly heat makes people come out their houses quick as roaches running off a hot stove. The front steps fill up then; so do the pavements and corners. The streets get busy with cars flying by, blasting music so loud it shakes windows and old people's bones too, I bet. Summertime is crazy time around here, my stepfather likes to say. "People lose their minds." I guess he knows how Philly heat can be, hot like cooked grits sliding down your back.

"The devil must have made Philadelphia," my stepdad says, pulling up his pants, "so he could vacation here in the summer, and not feel like he ever left home." His forehead is wet. So are his underarms, which stained his blue uniform already. His shirt is open, like all the windows in our house, but still don't cool him off none. It's eight a.m. the Fourth of July, and not just starting off hot; it's still hot from last night and the day before. Philly hot. "Give me another glass of water." He holds out a glass full of ice. "And fill up the pitcher in the fridge; a few jars, too. It's gonna be a bad one."

A bad one in Philly means a lot of things to a police officer like my stepdad, so I know he's not just talking about the heat. He's talking about all the things that can go wrong when heat and people who are sick and tired of the heat and everyone else all get mixed up together.

By the time I get back with the water, my stepsister Patricia is sitting in his lap, asking what she already knows the answer to. "Can we get us an air conditioner?" He hands her an ice cube. She rubs it over her forehead, under her arms, dripping water onto his pants. "They don't cost all that much."

She shouldn't mention money to him. He's cheap. And he's working two jobs, saving up for a new house. Him and Mom are always telling us that saving money for what we need is better than spending money on what we want. "Sacrifice," he says, patting her back so she will stand up and he can finish putting on his work boots. "We all gotta do it if we wanna get out of here."

Here is North Philly, where I was born—him and my mother too. They got married last year. Then we moved into this row house, which he says costs more rent money than it should for a house that crackheads used to sleep in. He stands up, stepping into another boot. Tying laces and stomping dirt off before shining his boots with a rag. "I gotta go. Y'all know the rules, right?"

I'm thirteen. I know the rules. I shouldn't have to repeat them to him every day before he leaves. I do anyhow, 'cause if I don't, well . . . I just do, that's all. "Stay inside. Clean the house. Don't answer the door. No BET or MTV. Drink water. Save the juice for supper. Look out for each other. Tell the bill collectors you sent the money in. Hit the floor if we gotta. And call you if things don't seem right."

He is almost out the door when our two-year-old sister comes into the living room kicking off her Pull-Ups and carrying a soggy undershirt. Golden's cheeks are as red as the mosquito bites she keeps scratching on her neck. My stepdad taped the holes in her window screen because he says we'll be moving soon and it don't make sense to buy new ones. But the bugs get to her anyhow. Picking her up is as easy for him as picking up chips off the floor. So before we know it she's on his shoulders, and he's telling her not to wet him before he goes to work. He kisses Golden and hands her to me. Then he hugs Patricia and shakes my hand. "They crazy 'round here. Lock up. Stay inside. I wanna find y'all alive when I get back." He's outdoors, saying hello to a neighbor, then listening while I put the locks on—one dead bolt, two chains, a latch, and a chair underneath the knob, just in case. Then he knocks to let me know I need to close some of the windows. I ignore that rule.

I keep looking out the window, making sure he gets that ride from Mr. Shabiz, just like he did yesterday. Then I'm picking up what my sisters threw down last night, thinking about the baths I got to give them, the lunch we have to get packed, the Kool-Aid I froze last night, and the kitchen floor that's got to be mopped, all before we three get dressed and go outside and have some fun in that Philly heat that my stepdad cannot tolerate.

It's bad enough to be hot in Philly; but to be hot and stuck inside should be illegal. So I move as fast as I can. Row houses catch the heat like frogs catch flies, and they hold on to it forever, the way graves hold caskets, Miss Evelyn said once. Besides, so much be happening out there, who wants to miss it? Only him, my stepdad, who don't love North Philly nearly as much as I do, and don't understand nothing about her neither.

Pop. Pop. Pow!
    Patricia ducks.
    Golden starts to cry.

I run into the street, watching firecrackers shoot over our house, turning silver, red, and blue.

"'Bout time." Elliott walks up to us. "Y'all late." He picks up Golden. "See what I got?" He hands a lit sparkler to her. "I'm ready to set something off."

I take it away from her. "Don't give her that."

He puts her down, reaches into his pocket, and pulls out his lighter and flicks. Elliott looks at fire like it's a girl he can't wait to kiss. I have to watch him. Last year he accidentally set his house on fire. The whole living room went up in flames. The couch, the bookshelf, his favorite chair—all gone. That's when I knew for sure you gotta keep six eyes on Elliott. It's the reason he don't come in my house no more either. Not because my stepdad says so, but because I say so. He might not mean to do it way deep down inside—but Elliott would fire something up in our place fast as you could turn on a light switch. And I like my sisters alive, and my bed just the way it is.

"Back up," he says. "Here go another one."

Before it's in the sky good, an ambulance flies past our block with its siren blasting. Two fire trucks follow behind it, horns beeping, sirens screaming, forcing drivers out their way. Elliott starts running. It's like the sirens are calling his name.

"Come on." He takes off after the trucks. "Let's see

where they go." He looks back at me, picking up speed when he sees I'm not moving.

I pick up a Blow Pop wrapper and then Golden and head for our porch.

My father's rules are like a rope tied around my hands and feet, forcing me to stay put even when I want to break loose, even when it looks like I am free to do whatever I like. *Watch them girls. Keep 'em inside. Be the man while I'm gone.*

I pull out juice boxes and straws. Twenty minutes later I'm still stuck, trapped outside in this Philly heat with two girls and a braid that won't stay plaited no matter how many times Golden asks me to redo it. "Let's go back in." Patricia wipes her sweaty forehead. "It's boring out here." She picks up a book and reads it to Golden when she sees me ignoring her.

Finally, Elliott comes back. "I couldn't catch 'em. But if we take the bus . . . that would be the quickest, fastest way."

I start packing up Golden. Patricia's eyes roll. "We don't wanna do that. It's hot." Her ankles cross so I know she ain't moving. "I'm telling Dad if you make us." She tells Golden not to move either. "Open the door so we can go in and watch cartoons."

My stepsister is like her dad. She don't like this Philly heat and she don't care for North Philly much either.

* * *

I didn't want to ditch 'em—that was Elliott's idea. But I could see my sisters weren't going to make it today. Philly heat ain't for everybody. Besides, Elliott reminded me, in three months it will be my fourteenth birthday. I've got to start acting my new age. "Dragging sisters around won't get you no girls," he says as we walk out of my cousin Danka's house. She's giving me three hours to hang out. "Any later and I'm feeding your sisters to the cats," she tells me.

You can sneak onto a bus in Philly, if you know how to. So when people get off the 32, Elliott and I go through the back door, crawling between legs and listening for the driver to tell us whether we've been caught.

We sit on the backseat, pushing open a broken window and sticking our heads out. Elliott yells to a girl wearing hardly anything. I watch the row houses go by, cats sitting under cars, cooling it, and girls with big thighs sitting on steps, using up their minutes. When someone wants off, the bus stops so hard that a woman who was standing ends up in some dude's lap. I would just let her sit there, if it was me. She's pretty. Dressed in a tan suit and wearing the kind of heels I like—red spikes.

"You smell that?"

I'm not sure if Elliott's talking about fire or barbecue. I smell 'em both.

When he jumps up and pulls the cord, I know which one he's talking about. You can eat anytime, but a fire you've got to catch when you can.

There's a crowd on the corner, watching. We can't see the flames, but we smell the smoke and hear firemen chopping doors and telling people to hurry out. "Excuse me. Sorry. Move." Elliott pushes his way to the front. His cell clicks more than mine did when I took pictures of my cousin going to the prom. He could stay here all day. Could watch a match burn all week. But fires bore me after a while, so I leave him and take off by myself.

Philly's got a lot of small blocks—mazes kind of. My stepdad says don't get caught on some of them after dark. But he's always looking at the bad side of things. They got murals in North Philly, too, the most beautiful in the world. I make my sisters stop whenever we see one, 'cause ain't no harm in appreciating something while you trying to run the streets.

All the houses on this block are knocked down, boarded up, or busted up. It's just me out here, smashing a SpaghettiOs can with my foot, putting it in my pocket, then climbing a tree that's growing smack-dab in the middle of a house, clear through the roof. A branch sticks out a third-floor window, like an arm through a sleeve. I get to the top of that tree and stare at the blue in the sky and everything down below, including cabbages growing in a yard next door, and pink roses climbing up a wall. I'm thinking about my sisters, wondering what my stepdad's gonna say when he finds out I ditched 'em. But I'm out, so I might as well stay out as long as I can and make it worth getting punished for, I figure.

"Let's go," I say, when I get back to Elliott.

He wants to stay. I take off without him, for good this time. You gotta do that with Elliott—just leave him. He likes to be in charge; to do everything his way.

Before I get to the end of the block, he's in front of me. "Look," he says.

One day Elliott's gonna get me killed. "Don't look. Keep walking." I'm trying not to look myself, but that's a whole lot of money they counting up on that porch. It's stacked as high as the red heels the lady wore on the bus.

Elliott stops. Not me. He heads for the porch. "What's up?"

The man in the black do-rag nods, looks at his dough, and says for Elliott to keep stepping. The woman on the porch with the missing railing stays on her knees, counting. She reminds me of my cousin, Tracie. Skinny. Smiling, but looking like she is sad from her eyebrows to her toenails.

Elliott's got this thing about him. He acts like he's

tougher than he really is. I think it's because of all the cops in his family—two uncles, a sister, one brother, and a grandfather. He ought to know better, because even Superman could get jacked up around here.

Elliott gets warned again. "Don't make me hurt you."

"He's slow," I tell the man. "Not right in the head."

He looks at the two of us. "So." He reaches inside his shirt and pulls out a shank.

Elliott has always been a fast runner. So he beats me to the end of the block. We turn the corner, roll past a man sitting on his porch, drinking beer and lotioning his wife's feet; almost run over a woman in a wheelchair riding up the middle of the street, carrying a rug and a floor lamp across her lap.

"Did you see it?" Elliott asks, walking backward. "All that money."

I stop to catch my breath. "You . . . wanna . . . die?"

He holds up the lighter and sets off a firecracker. "People 'round here know better. They touch me, they in jail for life."

Elliott first got the fire bug when he was six, he says, when his dad took him to a fire on South Street. It was big and went on for two days. People died. Some came out crying, with their clothes cooking and soot on their faces and their hair smoking, he told me. He felt bad for the people, but he fell in love with fire. "It made me feel happy like Christmas, not sad." Ever since, it's been in him to light and burn. His father tries to keep it a secret, but more and more Elliott says he can't keep it under wraps. "I gotta do it," he says, "like you gotta play Wii Sports every day."

Sometimes we walk and get nowhere. Sometimes we get lucky. We both are feeling lucky right now, because of the girl across the street. Everything about her makes us stare: her tight, short purple skirt; her little top; and those lips—pink, big, soft.

"Man." Elliott shakes his head. "Look at that," he says, tripping over the curb.

North Philly girls can do that to you: make you forget what you doing. The way they get their hair done. The way they dress like they going someplace special, when most likely they are just going around the block. How they walk like they got all day, but you don't mind because you ain't rushing to noplace nohow.

I'm standing on my toes because I want to see every piece of her. But then another girl walks up to the bus stop. Elliott and I look her up and down, 'cause when a North Philly girl walks by, it's like seeing one of them murals—something that don't just look good but makes you feel good way deep down inside too. "Sometimes . . . I think I'm never going to get a girl," I say.

Elliott wouldn't admit that even if it was true. He slaps his chest. "Shoot. Girls won't leave me alone."

He and I aren't the types that girls chase after. Or the kind they write notes to in class. Sometimes they call me "E" for "Ears." Elliott gets called other names. Goofy. Maniac. Firebug. Mouth.

I take another look at that girl. "Nice," I say, downing my soda, trying to cool off from this heat, and from that girl who is beautiful right down to the soles of her feet.

But we can't stare at girls all day. So we cut up one street and head down another, where some dudes are standing on the corner downing brew and playing craps. Elliott wants in. Not me. "Let's keep going."

He gets loud. "So what you gonna do when you fifteen, sixteen?" Elliott asks, like he's older than I am. "Still play video games? Basketball?" He crosses the street, flashing money. Dice hit the ground. Fingers snap. Hands slap, then stick out, waiting for people to pay up. I walk over too, because Elliott is right. I need to act my age. What do I ever do? Babysit. Collect trash. Who does that at my age? Nobody. I empty my pockets, dropping other people's trash on the ground.

"Lend me some money, Elliott."

Everyone here is older than us, in their twenties, mostly. They light up. Drink up. Cuss when they lose.

Cuss when they win. And get tired of Elliott and his mouth after a while. I notice things like that. Elliott never does. So I tell him that I need to take a leak, not because I have to, but because I hate the way they're talking to him—like he's someone you put up with but you really can't stand. A little while later, he's outta money anyhow. So we take off, before they run us off.

By the time we pass Spangler Street, my skin feels as hot as the plastic bottle I pick up off the ground and put in my bag. So when we see a swimming pool in front of a house, looking cool and clean, I stop.

"Let's get in."

No one's out on this block, just us. But we hear the family in the back, laughing and grilling. Elliott is out of his shirt and sneakers before I can change my mind. I kick off my sneakers. Let my shirt and pants hit the ground, then I slide into the water, staying underneath until my air is gone.

Rubber ducks and a beach ball, dead flies and a leaf float around us. Elliott does a headstand. I do a belly flop. He swims around the bottom, picking up pennies. It's a big pool, like maybe six feet deep. That's crazy. I never seen one this big sitting on a pavement before.

"Hey, Elliott, check this out." I dive in this time.

"Mom! They in our pool!"

I hear the words while I'm underwater.

"They stealing it!"

A broomstick gets me in the ribs. I pop up. "Hey! Don't . . ."

"Ouch!" Elliott holds his cheek. She smacked him with the bristles.

I'm limping, grabbing my sneakers and pants, telling him to bring the rest of our things. But then the father shows up. And he's got more than a broom with him.

You can not outrun a pit bull. But I'm trying.

We're running up the middle of the street, barefooted, wet, and in our underwear. "Help! Somebody . . ." I turn the corner, jump on the hood of a Merano, and climb onto the roof. "Elliott, run!"

Elliott hits the roof of a BMW so hard it dents. The dog puts its front legs on the fender; snaps and spits. People point. A man asks if we need help, but he don't move. A few minutes later, the owner walks up the block, whistling and waving to people he knows. "Lesson learned?" he says, putting a chain on the dog's neck.

Water is running down my legs, and it's not pool water. "Yeah," I say embarrassed.

"Wait till I tell my dad," Elliott yells at the man. "He's gonna kill you and your dog."

A door opens. A woman yells for Elliott to get off her

new car. "Now!" Then she runs down the steps, bare-footed. Elliott and I hit the ground at the same time, turning the corner so fast it's like we got wings instead of feet.

"This sucks."

Elliott looks at me.

"People been chasing us all morning." I pull up my pants. "I'm going home."

Two Muslim girls walk by in jeans and hijabs. "What if I got us some girls?"

"How you gonna do that? Girls don't like you, and they don't like me."

He follows them up the street, telling me to wait no matter how long he's gone.

I'm on Diamond Street; by the time he catches up to me it's half an hour later. He's got four girls with him—and they ain't ugly either. They're North Philly girls—fine. Walking slow and talking with their hands a lot. Smelling sweet and glossing their lips.

These girls, whose shorts are so tight and small I'd rather walk behind them than beside them, introduce themselves to me. Raven is shy, I think. She stares at the ground more than she looks up. That's my type—cute and quiet.

"There's a block party off of Ridge," Elliott says, putting his arms around Erista. "Let's hit that."

Philly loves block parties. You can find one anywhere in the summertime. So it doesn't take us long to find one. The street's blocked off, and all the cars are gone. Old ladies and fat girls line dance in the street. Men cook and cut cards. Little kids run up and down the block blowing bubbles, shooting water, and crying when they fall. The girl in front of me snaps her fingers and shakes her butt, then stops, drops, and pops. People laugh and run in and out of doors for more salt, spicy mustard, and lite beer. "I got next," a woman says, sitting down at a table to play tonk.

A boy my age stands up asking if anybody wants to play Pokeno. "For quarters, not nickels, though."

"Y'all eat?" a woman sitting out front her house asks. None of us knows her. She hands us plates. "Don't pass my house without eating something."

I pile my plate and dig in, eating everything I see— barbecued ribs and jerk chicken, potato salad, tuna salad, deviled eggs, and candied yams. At the next house I get watermelon, steak, and hot dogs. Then I stash empty M&M, Snickers, and Peppermint Pattie wrappers down my front pocket. Elliott tells me to chill when I pick up an empty pizza box, peeling off a piece of cheese that's still on it.

"Wipe your mouth," Jamilla says, patting my lips with a napkin.

I don't think Raven liked that.

We hit another block. Check out another party. It's hot and getting hotter. The deejay on the radio says it's ninety-seven degrees. "And we ain't done cooking yet."

Raven's nose sweats. Elliott's forehead is red. And me, well, the elastic around my drawers is soaking wet; so is the rest of me down there.

"We can go swimming," Elliott says.

"In what?"

The girls don't live far away, so they'll get their things, they say. It's Elliott and me that can't get into the local pool. But you know Elliott is nuts. He asks some people if they got old trunks or gym shorts that we can borrow. A woman who works at Sears, and lost her son in Iraq, feels sorry for us. She gives us trunks. And they fit.

North Philly girls got the best bodies, I swear. Karen and Jamilla don't have on blouses, only bikini tops with peep holes in the middle. Erista's got a chest big enough for two girls, and a butt as big as the moon. And even though Raven's suit is under her clothes, I'm thinking about how she's gonna look in it, and starting to sweat all over again.

"Check this out." Elliott's in front of a house that's just about burnt down. He's pulling Karen by the arm. She's giggling. Acting like she doesn't want to go in, but not fighting hard enough to stay out. I'm wondering about old needles, and rats. But she goes inside anyhow. When they come out, you can tell what happened. He got kissed. Her hair got messed up and so did her top. "Fix this," she says, asking her girl to retie the strings to her suit.

Raven looks at me. "Don't even think about it," she says, like I ever would.

We're outside the fence watching; smelling chlorine in the water and food cooking in the park across the way. People laugh and girls lie, telling guys, "Quit dunking me," then going back for more.

I sit by Raven on the edge of the pool, staring at her flat belly, wondering what she'd think if I picked up the pecan swirls wrapper or that Arizona Iced Tea empty and stuck 'em in my pants pocket. My stepdad hates when I do that. But I got my reasons.

Raven slides into the pool, one toe, one thigh, one arm at a time, like it's icy cold instead of warm as the sun. Dripping wet and smiling, she asks where I live and go to school. I forget about trash. I want to know if she has a boyfriend; what her cell number is. Not like I ask, though.

I get in and out of the pool talking to her, but making sure not to splash her hair, even though a little water finds it anyhow.

It's packed in the pool. So you can't help but bump into people. Since we came an hour ago, I accidentally knocked into this one dude like four times. I can't afford to do that no more.

But it happens anyhow.

"Quit it, man!" He's all muscles, like my stepdad.

"Sorry."

"Naw, man. You gotta do better than that."

He's like nineteen or twenty. Loud-talking me for swimming into him, 'cause too many people were around for me to do anything else. I walk away. He shoves me. Normally I would keep walking. But she's watching. "I *said* I was sorry! What you want me to do?"

"Yeah. What you want him to do?" It's Elliott. He is five-six and a hundred and ten pounds. No one is afraid of him. So the guy keeps talking to me.

He pulls his shorts up. "When I'm in the pool, you stay out the pool. Awright?"

"This my little brother. Don't talk to him like that." Elliott's got a big mouth.

The guy pushes me down and holds me under until water fills up my mouth. I come up coughing and spitting.

People circle us, looking at him and waiting for me to do something.

"You don't own the pool," I say.

Elliott's fists are up, but he gets pushed under the water, too, and held down a long time. Elliott is a fool. When he comes back up, he's still talking. "Do you know who I am? Do you know who my father is?"

The dude shoves him under again. Elliott comes up blowing snot into his hand and washing it off in the pool. Then out of his mouth comes the biggest lie. His father works for the DA, he says. And he pops off names to prove it. His mother is the mayor's secretary and his uncle is the assistant to the assistant chief of police. "You don't believe me, huh, huh?" Elliott is climbing out the pool. "Who got a cell? Hand me a cell!"

I don't know if the guy believes him, but the lifeguard comes over and asks what the problem is. He tells people to swim or get out. The guy who dunked us is underwater, at first. Then he pops up with a girl on his shoulders. She laughs. He throws her off and swims to the other side of the pool.

It's still not over when I get ready to leave.

Bam! I'm down on my knees.

"Don't swim near me no more," he says, diving back into the pool.

Elliott doesn't say a word. Neither do I. This is North Philly. This thing could go on until something even worse happens.

"You okay?" Raven wants to know.

The other girls are laughing.

My back burns so bad that I ask Elliott if he sees blood. "I think he used something," I tell him.

"Don't be like that in front of girls."

"Like what?"

He covers his mouth when he says it. "Like . . . lame."

I walk as straight as I can. But all I really want to do is sit down, before I fall down.

The girls spread out towels on the grass, then kicking off their flip-flops and sandals. Seals spit water at two little boys, while old men sit and play checkers. A half an hour more and then we'll leave, we all figure. Only Raven's friends take off before then. "Y'all boring," they say, leaving with their towels. I'm not sure why *she* stays. I wouldn't figure her to be the type to stick with two boys she hardly knows. We three stretch out in the hard, dry grass, listening to Michael Jackson singing on somebody's car radio, and water splashing. I close my eyes. Elliott asks her a question. I never hear the answer.

* * *

"How long we been asleep?" Raven wants to know.

The pool is closed, and the creeps are out. "I don't know. An hour?"

I tell her we'll walk her home. "Not till the fireworks are done, though," Elliott says, running up the hill and sitting down.

This is why I love North Philly. You can see all kinds of people and do all kinds of things—good or bad. Two Harleys ride up the middle of 33rd Street, side by side, doing wheelies and slowing traffic. Cars fly by in the opposite direction, beeping their horns at a man holding a sign saying HONK IF YOU'VE BEEN TESTED. Music loud enough to hear downtown makes one woman dance all by herself. She's throwing down so hard that a white dude jumps out his Volkswagen and finishes the song with her. Girls walk up the block in threes and tens. Cop cars creep up the street, watching, while reefer smells up the park and the homeless do their business in the dark.

I should go home. I'd tell Elliott that too, but she's here. And my stepdad is probably home, ready to shoot me. So I lay next to her and listen to the fireworks thunder and whistle, explode and pop, whiz nearby and shoot up high, then burst into a thousand stars.

As soon as it's over we run across the street. "Stop. Let's get some watermelon," she says. A man with a truck full of little ones gives us a sample. It tastes like sugar water, only sweeter. So we ask for more.

Elliott walks ahead of us, pointing at women painted blue and holding mics. Raven faces me. We walk and talk about the fireworks and melon, running out of conversation right in front of my favorite mural: a wall full of horses and people from around this way sitting tall on 'em. Golden always wants to ride on my back when she sees it, then we talk about all the places in the world she'll ride to one day. Raven tells me about the mural on 22nd Street. It's her favorite. "Somebody's gonna draw me on a mural one day," she says, posing. "Then I'll live forever."

Gunshots don't surprise us when we hear them. It's the Fourth of July weekend. Somebody's gonna die. "We better leave." I take her hand. She holds my fingers tight. I think I am the luckiest boy in the world.

Elliott is cool sometimes. While I walk Raven to her front door, he keeps quiet, mainly lighting matches and flicking 'em high in the air. I stare at her hard as I do those murals, because I know I won't ever see her again. She licks her pretty lips. I lick mine. She clears her throat. I do the same. Then a window opens. "Girl, get in here," her sister says. "Dad's looking for you."

Just like that, Raven's inside the house. Gone.

"You get her number?" Elliott asks.

"No."

"She wasn't that cute anyways."

It's what we say when we strike out.

We speed up, sweating like crazy. Philly heat don't know when to call it quits.

"He's gonna be mad," Elliott says.

I quit walking. "It was worth it. I didn't even notice the heat all that much. I mean, I met a girl. You can't meet a girl in the house with your sisters." We bump fists and I notice for the first time that him and me stink. I sniff my underarms. "You think she smelled me?"

"I smell you." His nose goes under both his pits. "But we always smell like this. What's the problem?"

Ain't no problem, I'm thinking, taking my time walking back home, watching fireworks shooting off of porches. "I had me the best time. Dag." I jump up, punching the air. "So I don't care. For real. What he say or do to me don't matter."

"Blame me." Elliott stops. "People blame me for everything anyhow."

My mother says Elliott's got sad eyes. They're not sad, just big and tired-looking, like he never sleeps, which is true. He's up till three every night. "Never could sleep," his mother always says. "Even when he was a baby."

"You gonna sleep good tonight," I tell him, yawning.

"As soon as he finishes yelling, I'm going to bed." I don't mention what I think next. That I'm going to sleep and kiss that Raven in my dreams.

Elliott turns in the opposite direction, jogs toward the corner. "Hold up. I'll be right back."

I pick up a Spicy Sweet Chili Doritos bag and two Hot Tamale boxes, flatten them and put them away. Our teacher said if we showed him what our neighbors were eating, he'd tell us what was eating our neighbors. He got sick and left for good back in May. But I'm still doing the project. Hot. Spicy. Sweet. That's what they like around here. I don't know what that means yet, but I'm gonna someday.

"Elliott!" I yell like he can hear me, then walk around the corner to find him. I'm in enough trouble already, I think.

I find him on the next street, sitting in a car somebody ditched, firing up trash. I don't know if he knows why he does it.

"Elliott!"

"I quit last summer."

"I know."

"But quitting only makes me think about it more." He takes the lighter and holds it to the busted leather seat with the stuffing pulled out.

"I know," I say, holding my hand out.

He adds more trash, trying to build a good fire. "If the whole car went up . . . man, that would be cool."

I look at him. "You take your medicine?'

He looks at me. "Naw."

My hand burns when I snuff out the fire. "What about yesterday? You take it then?"

He smiles. "It makes me sleep. All the time."

"You never sleep. That's your problem." I start walking. He jumps out the car and follows. "You got too much energy—up here." I point to his head. "Take the medicine. It's good food."

We laugh at that because his mom always says it. It's hard, I guess, being smart like him with a 130 IQ, but with a mind that won't do what he says.

"I ain't bad."

I take his hand. "Come on, we have to go."

He hands over the lighter, then digs in his pocket and gives me two more. "She was cute," he says, talking about Raven.

"Sure was. I shoulda asked for her number."

He slaps me on the back. "You gonna be fourteen soon. Not a kid no more. You better learn to ask." He digs in his pocket again and pulls out three numbers. "I do," he says, when we hit our block.

This is why I like Elliott. He's braver than I am. Funny and loyal, too. You can't give up on someone like that just because their mind don't work like yours.

There are police cars parked in front of my house. That ain't no surprise. We stop at the corner. I pick up an empty juice box and the top to a pack of Lemonheads.

"See you next year," Elliott says, crossing the street. "Hey. Happy birthday, early."

He's right. I'll be on punishment when my birthday comes in October.

"I'll get it for you. Her number, I mean."

Elliott and I would do anything for each other.

Everyone's outside, waiting for me; waiting for their houses to cool off too, I guess. Miss Evelyn's sitting on her steps, watching the news on TV. Four little flags hang in front of her house, drooping like her flowers. "Boy . . . when you gonna learn?" I stare at the screen. There's a reporter talking about a dead body they found, and there's a helicopter in the sky shining a light on another street.

Patricia and Golden run up and hug me. "You in trouble," Patricia says. "But I didn't tell."

One policeman is sitting in a car. The other one, Mr. Dave, is standing by the curb. "Hey, Mr. Dave," I say, watching him put his pad away.

"Where you been?" It's my stepdad.

Mr. Dave is my godfather. "This daggon Philly heat," he says, wiping his forehead. "It'll make you crazy." He looks at my father, while the other car pulls off. "Make a good boy do the wrong thing sometimes. Know what I mean?"

I tell them our house is hotter than fire. "We just wanted some air; water, too."

My stepfather grabs me by the front of the shirt. "I been calling the house all day. Danka finally told me how you left them girls and never came back." He asks what I was thinking, neglecting my sisters like that.

I push his hands away. "I'll be fourteen soon. I shouldn't be locked up in the house like you do them crooks!"

The people across the street get quiet. Patricia and Golden too.

My stepdad smells my breath. "I don't drink," I say, feeling Elliott rise up in me.

He pats my pockets.

"What you doing?'

"Empty 'em. Slow. One by one."

I've never ditched my sisters before. Never stayed out until dark. It's not right, him doing this to me. In public. And for what? Being a boy?

"Do you know how many people been shot tonight already?" He kicks my trash and asks my sister to pick it up. Sweat drips down his chin. "You know how many times I called home; rode around this neighborhood?" His fingers shake. And he stares at the ground. "Boys like you get into trouble 'round here all the time." He stands up straight and sends the girls inside to get something to eat. "I should . . ." His fist goes back. My eyes close.

Mr. Dave steps in between the two of us, and then walks a little ways with me. "When you're a father, you'll understand." He takes out a cigarette and lights it. "When you a cop, you know already. It's mean out here." He starts walking. "Don't make your father hurt you."

I try to explain.

"He will hurt you, if he thinks it's gonna keep them from hurting you," he says, pointing up the street. "Understand?"

"Yeah . . . but."

He tells me to shut up, then walks me over to my dad and says the two of us have to work it out. We sit outside, the three of us, talking. I try to tell them that I'm not a kid anymore. "You lock me up, I'm gonna bust out—anybody would." I'm shaking while I'm saying it, because once Mr. Dave is gone, my stepdad will show me who's really in charge. But I don't care. I met me a girl. I ate me the best food. And I'm never gonna forget those fireworks and her sleeping next to me.

My stepdad stares at his boots. "I told you . . ."

"I know."

"If you got hurt . . . if the girls got hurt . . ."

My godfather asks to speak to him a minute. They go inside and come out shaking hands and talking about how hot it is. Mr. Dave goes back to work. My stepdad gets back to me. "I'm never gonna understand you liking North Philly the way you do." All he sees is the trash, and kids out of control, police trying to get people to talk who won't, and boys like me in trouble or dead. But if he saw Raven. If he had that lady's sweet potato pie, or if he saw all that money on the porch, or those people line dancing, and grilling in the dark, then he'd know why I love North Philly.

He opens the door. "Maybe we need to change a few things around here." He picks up Golden, who is out of her Pull-Ups again. "But first you have to get what's coming to you." He's quiet a minute. "Tell me what you think is fair—and don't be messing around, 'cause I got plenty ideas about how to make you wish you were never even born."

I look at him standing there like a mountain in that doorway. He doesn't wait for an answer. He walks into the house asking Golden if she wants Ernie in the tub with her, or Mickey Mouse.

I don't know why, but he doesn't tell me to come inside. And I don't go, not for a while, anyhow. I sit. I tell my stomach to quiet down when I smell fish frying up the street somewhere. I watch my neighbors kicking back, talking on cells and to each other. I hear Miss Bert yelling to someone to bring her a bowl of butter pecan ice cream, and some grease, so she can oil her scalp.

Philly heat. It makes people stay outdoors all night long. You can't hardly sleep for the heat and the noise sometimes. That's why I like it, though—like living here, feeling the heat, watching people walking the streets—knowing that it ain't all bad; ain't all good, neither. It's just where I live. My hood.

WORDS TO THE WORLD

Brown
Baby
Girl
Beauty of the world
My little sis
Here's another kiss
A poem
A hug
Words to show the world
Just how much you're loved

I APOLOGIZE

I apologize
For living in the suburbs,
For talking white,
For trying to be cooler than I am,
For locking my windows when my mom drives me
    into the city at night,
For choosing Harvard over Howard,
For not going to public school,
For taking Paige to the prom,
And for sitting up in church, singing hymns like life
    was ever hard for me.
I apologize
For that time I pretended not to see you cutting up,
Or the time I sat in the barbershop, scared that more
    than my hair was going to get cut.

I apologize
For looking like you, but not knowing exactly who you
    are.
But you can apologize too, you know.
I hear you laughing at the way I speak,
Pointing at the geek you say is me walking up the
    street,
Asking why my family gotta act so white.
Stepping up to me because you think I can't fight.
I know what happens when I show up at a dance:
You and your boys sit back and don't give me a
    chance.
Laughter happens whenever you see me around,
Unless you need to borrow some money.
Then, well, of course me and you is down.
I don't always understand you.
You don't seem to get me at all.
I prefer golf,
You swear by basketball.
We are
City
And
Suburb,
A million miles apart.
Brothers

Still trying to understand and forgive one another.
So I apologize
For whatever.
And you?

PRETTY MOTHERS ARE A PROBLEM

THE DAY SHE MOVED into our building, I was just about to hook up with my friend Sedgley to sell some weed. Money is tight. Mom's check got cut back 'cause my little brother went to live with my dad. I did the best I could—making cheese steaks at Big Willie's on the weekends, sweeping up at JT's gas station Wednesday and Thursday nights. But the economy sucks, so they both let me go, then hired their relatives to take my place.

When you fifteen, they want to pay you like a boy. But Mom says I eat like a man; got man-size feet too—elevens. So I need to make some real dough. Sedgley and his boys always got plenty of money, so I was all set to make a run with him when I saw *her* outside our building. I had to speak 'cause she caught me checking out her mom— eyeballing her butt, to be honest. Her mom had on this short, tight jean skirt; no slip, no stockings, and long legs that went on forever. I could feel my cheeks turn red, so I apologized, something my boys tell me I need to quit doing. But it's not cool checking out some girl's mom. So after I said I was sorry, I picked up a box and carried it inside.

Her mom stopped me when I came for the second one. "This here's Ashlee," she said, smiling. She took the snake plant off Ashlee and told her to "Say hello to the boy." Ashlee didn't say a word. So her mom stuck out her hand and said, "You can call me Aretha."

Ashlee kept taking things out of the U-Haul and into apartment 3B, across the hall from me and Mom. She was pretty, like her mom, but you could tell she wasn't nothing like her mom, who had a pierced eyebrow, three tattoos on her left arm, the prettiest legs I ever seen. And she switched so hard the mailman across the street stopped working for like ten minutes just to watch her walk up the apartment steps, and in and out of the building.

Ashlee's mom was young, like my mom. She was maybe thirty-two. "How old did you say you were?" Aretha asked me. I told her seventeen. Then she asked about my mom. "When I meet her I'm gonna let her know what a gentleman she raised." She pinched my cheek. I picked up two more boxes—big ones. And I thought about Sedgley, who was probably mad at me right then. I was supposed to make a few runs with him last week, too. But I chickened out.

I'm a hard worker. Everyone knows that. Once I get started, watch out, I'm gonna outwork everyone else around me. Ashlee was the same way. She carried heavy boxes, two and three chairs at a time. Her mom was different. Aretha don't mind letting someone else do all the work. The first half hour I was there, she took two breaks—one to fix a broken nail, the other to drink a glass of cherry Kool-Aid. She made a production out of everything too. She didn't just gulp down the Kool-Aid like us guys do: she used a straw. She lotioned her legs, sipped Kool-Aid, put on lip gloss, sipped, talked on the cell, chewed on ice, and asked Ashlee over and over again: "How my lips look? My legs ashy? This outfit okay?" I'm glad she did not ask me.

"Quit it."

I ain't sure if Ashlee was talking to me or her mom. I don't think I was staring at her legs. But who knows, maybe she saw her mom looking me over. Sedgley says that older women like me, even though he can't figure out why. I don't think they like me like that, it's just that they're all single around here mostly, and there ain't no one to help 'em out but me.

"Quit fooling around, Mom," Ashlee said. "Or we're never getting done."

Aretha asked if I had some friends who could maybe help us move things along. I said I'd call around. But I know my friends. They wanna get paid, and Aretha wasn't the type to give up cash. She was used to people doing for her just because, I could tell.

She winked when she thanked me. Then she left the room. I kept my eyes on the floor, but I thought about her. Older women. Young dudes. My mom would say there's something wrong with that.

I can tell when a girl doesn't want me around. So I stayed outside when Ashlee was inside, and left when she came in the apartment to do something. Ashlee was not friendly like her mom. She ain't say one word to me. I asked what school she went to. Nothing. Asked how old she was and why nobody was here to help 'em out. She kept her lips tight. That ticked me off, you know. So I called Sedgley. Told him I was on my way. He said to forget it. Then the phone went dead.

"I gotta go," I told Aretha, when I got outside. She handed me another box, then asked if I could carry in just one more little thing—a love seat. Maybe it was the way she said it. Or maybe it was the way she looked. But I carried it inside, then took another love seat in too. I just about busted my back doing it. And when I came out, feeling kinda good about what I did, that Ashlee still ain't say nothing to me.

She was sitting on the steps, looking up and down the block. "I'm not moving no more."

I didn't know why she was saying that to me. Then I saw who she was talking to.

Aretha was in the window, taking another cigarette break. She promised Ashlee this was the last move. I don't think Ashlee believed her. This was the third move this year, Ashlee reminded her. It was her second school; the third bus route she had to learn. "Things happen," her mom said.

Ashlee was upset. "Most people live in the same house all their lives. They . . . just forget it, Mom," she said, jumping up, pushing past me when she went inside. Before I knew anything, though, she was right back out there with us. "We need more help. Who's gonna move that couch? Him? And what about the beds? And the TVs?" Ashlee wasn't waiting for answers. She was gone again.

It was like two sisters arguing. "This is why you always by yourself, Miss Mean and Nasty," her mom said. But instead of going to talk to Ashlee, Aretha came out and sat down next to me. "You sure you can't stay longer?"

I needed to go. But I didn't want to. She was pretty. And she didn't have no other guy to help her out. So I offered to stick around. I got a kiss on the cheek for that. My friends would say I was lucky, getting kissed by a woman like her. But it was kind of weird when I stood up and saw Ashlee standing in the front door, staring.

"That's my mother," she said, then walked away.

Ashlee looked really sad, so I was gonna apologize, but my mom come out.

"How you doing, baby?" my mother said, massaging my shoulders.

"Mom! Don't do that."

My mother laughed. "Don't want your friends to know I still give my baby back rubs?" she said, pinching the same cheek that Aretha kissed.

I was glad to see my mom, but not happy with that top she had on. I quit getting on my mom about her clothes a long time ago, though. She never listens anyhow. And after a while your boys stop making comments, out of respect for you, I guess. Or maybe they just feel sorry for you—having a mom who still thinks she's nineteen; partying and dressing that way too. "I'm grown," Mom always says. But I think I'm more grown, responsible, than her sometimes. It's like she's my sister, not my mom. But she don't seem to get that.

Aretha cuts her eyes at me, then at my mom, checking her out.

"Mom, this is Aretha . . . and Ashlee," I say when Ash walks onto the porch.

My mom wanted to know if Aretha could sing. It was a joke: Aretha said she got that all the time. I watched them, compared them. And I could see, a little, how my boys felt about my mom. I mean, Aretha is fine . . . built. I wouldn't want to be Ashlee. I could tell if they walked down the street together who would get all the looks and whistles. My mom is like that—a dude magnet. So I knew her and Aretha would hit it off. But Mom didn't see how Aretha was looking at me—like I was a man. I got up then and went to the truck and worked until my arms hurt.

Women talk a lot. I'm used to that. But they should watch who they spend their time talking to. Mom and Aretha were talking to Mr. Dorsey. They were leaning over the railing, smoking cigarettes and crossing their legs. His eyes went from one woman to the other.

"You helping us, or what?" I asked him.

Mr. Dorsey looked over at me. "We still got beds to bring in," I told him.

My mom stood up. Aretha crossed her arms and winked at me. "We could use some extra hands," she told Mr. Dorsey. "I'm frying up chicken once we're done."

Mr. Dorsey is like a lot of guys. He'll talk to a woman. Flirt with a woman. But he won't do any work for a woman. "What time is it?" he said.

Time to go, I thought. It was, too. He said he was off to get his hair cut. And he was gone before they knew it. I was glad. I think Aretha was too. Ashlee was different. She was still mad about things. And every once in a while she just stared at me. Then she'd look at her mom and kind of shake her head. Pretty mothers are a problem; me and Ashlee both know that.

My mother likes shoes. So does Aretha, it turned out. She had boxes and boxes of them. The two of them took in the shoes. Aretha has the only apartment with three bedrooms in it. The smallest room was going to be her shoe room, she said. And once the two of them got back there, they stayed awhile. It turned out they wore the same size shoe. And Aretha was like my mom, generous. So she offered to lend her a few pair. Before you knew it, my mom was in and out of our apartment with dresses that went with Aretha's shoes. I was in the kitchen, putting dishes in the cabinet. Ashlee was handling the silverware. In came our moms, dressed like they were going clubbing. Ashlee looked at me. We both looked at them. Then went right back to work.

I don't know, maybe it's because it's mostly been me

and my mom, but I got a way with women. I know how to cheer 'em up. So I told Ashlee about the time I took four of my mother's dresses and burned them in the yard. "They looked like T-shirts, they were so short."

She laughed. "If I did that, she wouldn't have any clothes."

"They don't mean any harm," I said, thinking about the dresses they had just put on. My mom was not ever going out in that thing. Hot pink looks good on her. But it's like a sign. She wears it and men stick to her like a stinger in your finger. It's cut too low here and up too high there. But Aretha's dress—wow. I couldn't say that to Ashlee, but man. Wow. I could see why they probably had to move so much. A woman like that can't stay put too long. Other women get mad, I bet. Men get stupid, most likely talking to her a little too much; stopping by for sugar or something else sweet. "Where's your dad?"

"Who knows?"

I looked at Aretha, going out the front door to get more shoes from the van. I would never walk away and leave a woman like her. Just like I wouldn't leave my mom. They the kind that need a good man. Somebody to keep the losers away.

"Malik," she said, walking back and coming into the kitchen, "you okay?"

I stood up. "Yeah."

"You sure we ain't working you too hard?"

I shook my head no.

"What you want, Mom?" Ashlee said.

"Just thinking," she said.

She was thinking about me. I knew it. But she lied. She told Ashlee she was thinking about the curtains she had bought. She was having second thoughts about the color. I wasn't having second thoughts. I wasn't feeling guilty either, about me being young and her being my mother's age. I'm mature. Everyone says so. I could date an older woman, I thought, watching her walk out the room. Listening to her talk to my mother about what a fine young man I am.

"You lying," Sedgley said, when I saw him the next day. "You don't even shave. She don't want you." He looked up at her place. "Introduce me."

Sedgley is older than I am. Eighteen. "A boy like you won't know what to do with that."

I was in his car, sitting outside my front door. It was lunchtime. We still hadn't finished unpacking the truck. . . . But Aretha is like my mother—don't wake her up before twelve thirty on Saturdays.

"I'm telling you, man. I think she likes me."

We headed up 62nd Street. A few minutes later the

speedometer was hitting ninety. He talked to me about older women. He'd dated a lot of them, mostly ones in their thirties and forties. "They the best kind," he said. "Desperate, with plenty of dough."

"Money?"

"You have to get the dough. Otherwise, what's the point?" He thought about that. "Here's how you handle older women," he said, trying to school me. And before I got out the car he dropped a buck-fifty on me. "You can't do the streets," he said, telling me to forget trying to make runs with him. "But if you play your cards right with her, you might get paid anyhow."

When Sedgley dropped me off, my mom and them were outside working. He looked at Aretha. He looked at me. "Nice," he said, licking his lips.

Sedg and I used to go to school together. He dropped out the last half of his last year in high school. "Money," he said. "That's all you need to make it in America." I looked at Aretha when Sedgley drove off. I didn't want her money. She's like my mom—she doesn't have much. But I could see being with a woman like her.

My mom usually notices things. But she couldn't tell that something was going on between Aretha and me. I helped Aretha take in the dining room table. All four of us put the legs on. We all helped bring in the china cabinet too. Aretha's shoes were high. Not the kind you wear when you move in someplace. The kind you'd wear if you wanted someone to notice you. I noticed. Some guys on the block did too. But they wasn't out there helping her. I was. So I got mad that she stopped whenever they wanted to introduce themselves.

"Aretha! I don't have all day," I said.

Ashlee dropped a box on my toe. I think it was on purpose.

Aretha knows how to get guys to do things she wants. She kissed me on the cheek. "I'm ready," she said, taking me by the hand, ignoring Mom and Ashlee.

"Alright now, you too old for my baby," Mom said, joking. Then she kissed me on the other cheek.

That just messed everything up, though; made me feel kind of guilty for what I was thinking. "Hey, Ash . . . let me get that for you," I said, picking up the box. She rolled her eyes and went inside.

Pretty women spend a lot of time trying to get guys to look at them. My mother and Aretha do that. During a break, they sat on the steps smoking. They crossed their legs at the ankles and talked loud. So of course guys stopped. They gave them compliments and even asked for Aretha's phone number. I stood behind her then. "Naw, I don't think so," she said, twice.

"I told you," my mom said. "That boy thinks he's my husband—yours too now."

Aretha leaned way back, looking at me standing behind her. "I never had a husband," she said. "I don't think I'd know what to do with one."

"I had one. We know what to do with them, huh?" Mom said, looking back at me.

My father had another family that he never told us about. They lived in Denver; we lived here. Once Mom found out, she left him. We just get by on the money she makes working at the Dollar Store. I'd never be that kind of man, I tell her. And I couldn't be what Sedgley said I should be either. Someone to take a woman's money.

"You're tall," Aretha said. "Come inside and help me get something off that top shelf."

The guy on the pavement looked up. Then smiled at me. "Lucky," I heard him say.

"What you talking about?" Mom asked.

He told her about the lottery number he was thinking of playing. I follow Aretha, wondering what she would do if I kissed her. I mean, I could, if Ashlee and my mom weren't around.

"Stand here." She pulled a chair up to the breakfront. "Hold it steady."

She held on to my shoulder. Put one foot on the chair and then the other. "Don't let me fall."

I held on to her waist while her arms stretched and grabbed a glass punch bowl. "Now why did I want this?" she said, giggling.

I looked behind me for Ashlee, who was in the kitchen when we walked through. I listened for my mother. And when Aretha stepped off the chair without the bowl, I pulled her to me. Neither one of us moved. We just stared at each other. I've kissed a couple of girls before. I knew what to do. But she wasn't a girl. She was a woman.

"Well?" she said.

It was like getting a PlayStation 3 and just staring at the instruction book. So she kissed me; hard.

"That's my mother!"

Ashlee looked at her mom. "You make me sick." She ran out the room.

My mother's gonna kill me, I thought.

Aretha wiped lipstick off my mouth. "She won't tell," she said, going to find Ash. "She won't."

I just stood there thinking about my mother.

The door to Ashlee's room slammed. I heard them arguing inside. Ashlee was asking how Aretha could do something like that to her again. Again? I thought.

"You're old!" she said. "And that's . . . that's like, abuse."

Aretha blamed it on me. Said I helped her up, then I kissed her. "You know how young boys get around me."

"I know how *you* get around boys," Ashlee said. "You almost went to jail for that before, you know."

"Ashlee!"

"What if some old man did that to me?" The door opened, then slammed shut again. "What if I found me somebody old as dirt? Like some of those weirdos who come up to me sometimes."

"I ain't old!"

"That's the problem," she said. "You think you my age. You think you're a teenager. You're grown. So grow up!"

The door opened. My mother walked into the house. Ashlee ran out her room, crying. "What's wrong?" my mother wanted to know.

"Nothing," all three of us said.

My mom always says she wasn't born yesterday. "Ashlee, what happened?"

Ashlee looked at me. Then she looked at her mom. *Ask them*, I thought she would say. But she just walked out the house.

We went to the door behind her.

She walked up the street.

My mom said Aretha better go after her. "She don't know her way around here."

Aretha said that Ashlee was the type that needed time to cool down. "She'll be back," she said, walking into the U-Haul. "Let's just finish up."

I was worried about Ashlee, but mostly I was thinking about that kiss. If Aretha wanted me to remember it, she did a good job. The whole time we were unloading I thought about it. You get to be good at things by practicing. I wondered how many guys she had practiced on. How many were my age?

"Ashlee can be so dramatic," she said, taking blankets into the apartment.

"Him too," Mom said. "Just don't let him get his way. He pouts." She stopped and squeezed my lips together.

"Don't do that."

"He's my baby, though," she said, blowing me a kiss.

"Mom. Don't." I looked over at Aretha.

"Boys do like their moms, now, don't they?" Aretha said.

We walked upstairs and into Ashlee's room. "Girl, I would kill somebody over this boy," my mom said.

Aretha cut her eyes at me.

"He ain't never give me no trouble." Mom talked about some of her friends and their kids. "I'm the troublemaker in this family," she said, laughing. "He has to keep me in line."

She told Aretha about the time I made her quit

working at the bar. And that day some dude she was dating thought it was okay to beat up on her. "He a blessing," she said. "But when he gets married, I'm not sure his wife is gonna like him trying to boss her around."

I took the blankets and put them up high. My mom walked out of the room first. Then Aretha. Then me. Her hands were behind her back. One reached out to me. I wanted to grab it, hold on to it. But my mom might've seen, and boy, it would be on then. She'd kill Aretha over me.

They almost called the police on Ashlee—my mom did, anyhow. Aretha seemed okay with her coming in after midnight. That was a few weeks ago. It's like Aretha dropped me after she got all moved in. Or maybe it was because of Ashlee. She hasn't spoken to me since.

"Listen," my mom says, putting her makeup on. "I'm going out. Aretha was supposed to go with me, but she canceled at the last minute."

I still think about her. Bump into her in the hallway sometimes. She smiles, but that's it.

"When you coming back?" I ask my mom. I fasten her necklace. "Who you going with? You got a ride?"

"A couple of girls I work with gonna be there. Somebody will bring me home." She buttons her blouse and reminds me to eat the rest of my dinner. Then she says, "How do I look? Skirt too short? Blouse okay?" she says, kissing me. "Love you. Anything go wrong, you have the cell number."

An hour later she's walking out the door. I'm watching television, listening to music, when I hear another door shut. I've been watching Aretha, standing in the hall sniffing her perfume after she leaves in the morning for work. Sedgley says be patient, she's not done with me yet. "But don't be no fool. She your mom's age. She don't want you around for long."

I open the kitchen window. It's her. I hear her talking. I hear a guy too. They're on the porch.

I listen for Ashlee, because I still avoid her. Then I walk down the steps. It's a free country, I tell myself. I can sit on the porch if I want.

"There's your husband," Mr. Dorsey says. "Or is he your boyfriend?"

Aretha laughs. "Please."

Mr. Dorsey sounds serious. "Don't get yourself into no trouble with the law, girl."

She looks over at me. "He's Ashlee's friend." She winks at me, then turns back to him. "So, what were we talking about?"

I sit there listening to her flirt with him. I smell the

cigarette smoke and see her legs, shiny from the lotion she uses, with the glitter in it. I should leave. But I stay, staring at him the whole time. Every once in a while he looks at me and says, "That boy like you."

"You think? Naw," she says, walking over to the railing and asking him for a light.

I get a good look at her. And I swear she keeps looking over her shoulder at me. If she was my mother, I'd tell her that skirt is too short and her top shows a little too much. If she were my girl . . . I stare at my feet. Sedgley says don't ever think of older women as yours. "They like some dudes. They trying to have fun, not go to the prom with you."

"Bye," I say, making sure they both hear me. It's not too late. I think I'll hook up with some of my friends, so I go inside for my cell and my money.

She's by herself on the porch when I finally come back out.

"Hey."

I keep walking.

"Malik."

I look over at her.

"Sit."

It's a command, not a request. I don't like it when my mother does that. But I sit at the other end of the lounger.

"I ain't mean to give you the wrong impression."

Sedgley said she just used me to help her move in.

"I ain't that kind of person." She moves closer to me.

I stand up. Then sit back down. "Miss Aretha."

"Aretha," she says, giving me that smile. "I ain't that much older than you."

She lights another cigarette and blows smoke in my face for a really long time. I hate smoke, but I breathe in as much of her as I can. "Your mom, there's some things she shouldn't know, you know?"

I look at her.

"Ashlee either," she says, putting her finger up to her lips, standing and holding her hand out to me. "Not all secrets are bad," she says, offering me a smoke.

I look up at her. At the cigarette, then the door. My mother would kill me, I think, staring at the cigarette.

OPEN YOUR EYES

When you see me,
See me.
It's the least that you can do.

If You Need to Talk to Someone

About unplanned pregnancy
American Pregnancy Helpline
1-866-942-6466

The Religious Coalition for Reproductive Choice
1-202-628-7700
info@RCRC.org

About thoughts of suicide
USA National Suicide Hotlines
Toll-Free / 24 hours / 7 days a week
1-800-SUICIDE (1-800-784-2433)
1-800-273-TALK (1-800-273-8255)
1-800-799-4889 (TTY)

About sexual abuse

1-800-656-HOPE (1-800-656-4673)

About HIV/AIDS

CDC National AIDS/Sexually Transmitted Disease Hotline

1-800-232-4636 (English)

1-800-232-4636 (Spanish)

1-888-232-6348 (TTY)

8 a.m. to 8 p.m. ET, Monday through Friday

About violence at home

loveisrespect, National Teen Dating Abuse Helpline

1-866-331-9474

1-866-331-8453 (TTY)

If you liked this book, you will also enjoy

Who Am I Without Him?
Short Stories About Girls and the Boys in Their Lives
by Sharon G. Flake

"Written in the vernacular of urban African-American teens, which Flake captures flawlessly, these 10 stories have universal themes and situations. Some are funny and uplifting; others, disturbing and sad. Addressing issues and situations that many girls face in today's often complex society, this book is provocative and thought-provoking."
   —*School Library Journal*

★ "Hilarious and anguished, these 10 short stories about growing up black today speak with rare truth about family, friends, school, and especially about finding a boyfriend. The stories work because Flake never denies the truths of poverty, prejudice, and failure."
   —*Booklist* (starred review)

Coretta Scott King Author Honor Award
Booklist Editor's Choice Award
Booklist Top 10 Romance Novels for Youth
YALSA Best Books for Young Adults
YALSA Quick Picks for Reluctant Readers

Praise for SHARON G. FLAKE

THE SKIN I'M IN
Winner of the Coretta Scott King / John Steptoe Award
for New Talent

New York Public Library Top Ten Books
for the Teen Age

★ "Flake's debut novel will hit home."
—*Publishers Weekly* (starred review)

BANG!
ALA Best Books for Young Adults

VOYA Top Shelf Fiction

"Disturbing, thought-provoking."
—*School Library Journal*

WHO AM I WITHOUT HIM?
Coretta Scott King Author Honor Book

★ "Honest and valuable."
—*Kirkus Reviews* (starred review)

★ "Hilarious and anguished, these twelve
short stories . . . speak with rare truth."
—*Booklist* (starred review)

YOU DON'T EVEN KNOW ME
The companion to *Who Am I Without Him?*

"These complex and thought-provoking stories won't disappoint."
—*School Library Journal*

"The immediate voices . . . are well-suited for readers' theater and for sharing everywhere."
—*Booklist*

MONEY HUNGRY
Coretta Scott King Author Honor Book

Los Angeles Times Recommended Book for Teens

★ "Razor-sharp dialogue . . . a story that's immediate, vivid, and unsensationalized."
—*Booklist* (starred review)

BEGGING FOR CHANGE
The sequel to *Money Hungry*

An ALA Quick Pick

A *Bulletin* Blue Ribbon Book

★ "Flake's charged, infectious dialogue will sweep readers through the first-person story . . . Hopeful."
—*Booklist* (starred review)

Sharon G. Flake's breakout novel, *The Skin I'm In*, established her as a favorite among middle and high school students, parents, and educators worldwide. She has spoken to more than two hundred thousand young people, and hugged nearly as many. Her work—nine novels, numerous short stories, plays, and a picture book entitled *You Are Not a Cat*—has been translated into multiple languages, including French, Korean, and Portuguese. She is the recipient of numerous awards, such as the Coretta Scott King Honor and the YWCA Racial Justice Award, and her books have been named to many prestigious lists, including *Kirkus Reviews*' Top Ten Books of the Year, Best Books for Young Adults by the American Library Association, Top Ten Books for the Teen Age by the New York Public Library, Top Twenty Recommended Books to Read by the Texas Library Association, and *Booklist* Editor's Choice, among others. She lives in Pittsburgh, Pennsylvania. For more information, go to sharongflake.com, or follow her on Twitter @sharonflake.